BAD BLOOD

Bad Blood
(Blood Rights, Book One)

K. B. Thorne

To the citizens of Night Haven and the writers who brought them to life.

You helped me make Adelheid what it is today, and I hope that those characters who were inspired by yours do you justice now.

CHAPTER ONE

That's the part about being a vampire that I've always hated.

The perks are great, but lunch can kill you...and I'm not talking 'I can't believe I ate the whole thing' kind of kill you, either. I mean, pull a wooden stake out of their back pocket and murder you.

Now, let's be clear about something. I wasn't actually trying to eat anybody or even planning to eat anybody when the blonde psycho came flying out of the forest and drove a stake into my chest. Here I am, just trying to make an honest living, when some whack-job with a slayer complex comes darting out of the shadows and decides that I'm the one responsible for every crime committed by supernaturals over the past several centuries in reality and in fiction. Basically, I was assaulted over *Dracula*.

Fortunately for me, the psycho had bad aim and got closer to my shoulder than my heart so my undead ass remained undead rather than totally dead.

This turn of events was bad enough, but I could handle it. What was more of a struggle for me to deal with was the hysterics.

No, I'm not talking about my hysterics. I wasn't hysterical. In fact, given the circumstances, I was quite calm. I'm talking about my clients. While I'm sure that having their preternatural expert-adviser-type person skewered wasn't in their original plan, I was walking and talking, so was it really necessary to carry on like that? Vampire hearing is *very* sensitive, so wailing and shrieking really hurts. Wasn't I in enough pain already?

"Mrs. White, please, really, I'm okay. Calm down," I said through clenched teeth. My hand was pressed against the wound, holding back the oozing tide until I healed.

If it hadn't been for my clients—yes, even with the screaming—I probably would have gone after the bitch and said shoulder-be-damned, but I had a responsibility to the people who hired me... Besides, I was a little impaired.

"But then...she just...out of nowhere...blood..." Mrs. Regina White sputtered, as if *she'd* been the one stabbed, before she promptly fainted.

Ernest White, who I assumed was her husband although no one had actually said it, knelt beside her in a panic and then glared at me. This wasn't my fault. I didn't sign up to get stabbed, you know?

I managed to keep my mouth shut on that, however.

Fifteen minutes later, I was sitting on the hood of my car. I had little patience for theatrics but didn't quite feel free to leave, so this seemed like a good compromise. My hyper-physical body had healed the wound, although the blood drying on my skin and shirt was kind of gross.

Ernest was walking towards me, and I rather dumbly got a little nervous. I mean, I knew I could take him in any sort of fight, fair or otherwise, but it was the stress factor I was worried about. Tonight wasn't really doing great things for me.

"Miss Stanton," he began, wringing his hands.

I wanted to correct him and tell him to call me something else, but the truth was that I didn't really have a title. Still, for some reason, 'Miss' Stanton just sounded wrong.

He continued, "I'm terribly sorry about Regina. She just

doesn't handle surprises very well."

I managed not to comment about the fact that this had been a much bigger surprise for *me* than for her.

"I'm sure," I replied as sympathetically as I could manage.

I try to be a nice person, but my shoulder hurt like hell, and I just wanted to leave.

Maybe I should introduce myself.

My name is Sadie Stanton. I'm the owner of the Stanton Agency. We serve the community in all matters preternatural, and we specialize in helping the preternatural community, and we had been doing it for... Well, if we were lucky, we'd be looking at a whole year. I started the business not long after the institution of Cameron's Law, which made all supernatural beings legal citizens. I felt that we needed a place where people could come for paranormal services, and where the supernatural could come for help.

As the boss, and one of the only employees, I had the joy of doing a little of everything. I was in charge of myself and could work any million hours a week I wanted, provided they were without sunlight.

Tonight, I was at St. Gertrude's Cemetery on Wallace Street on a job that was a little closer to the peripheries of my abilities, but I could do it, and it paid my bills.

Ernest and Regina White had buried her father two weeks before and for some reason, they were afraid he was going to wake up as a vampire, or that he already had. As for the first one, I could count it out. If he hadn't yet, he wasn't going to. As for the second, well, that was why we were standing in a cemetery at midnight.

As a vampire, I have some sense of other vampires and of the dead. I had just been kneeling on the grave, sensing the presence of a fully human and decomposing body beneath me, and was getting to my feet when the psycho came out of the tree line three graves to my right and did the aforementioned stabbing. Now that things were a little calmer, I remembered that I should probably deliver the good news.

"Mr. White," I said, still trying to smile. "Before we were interrupted, I had been about to tell you that your father-in-law remains in his grave, very dead, very human. You don't have anything to worry about." I was making a guess on the father-in-law part, but he didn't complain so I figured my guess was right. Good for my powers of deduction.

The look of relief on Ernest's face made me wonder what he thought his father-in-law would actually do if he was up and walking again. Perhaps there wasn't much peace with the in-laws, or maybe he just didn't like vampires. Either was possible, but I wasn't about to ask. It wasn't my business and right then, I didn't really care.

Being a dutiful husband, he thanked me and headed over to where his wife was leaning against a headstone, fanning herself. He apparently gave her the good news, because she then also looked relieved and fainted again. I shook my head and slid off the hood, giving them a little wave as I got in the car. My part of the job was finished, so I was leaving.

Being stabbed really takes it out of a girl.

☾ O ☽

Once in my car, I scrounged around for anything that might be useful. I found one of those wet wipe packets you get with a messy dinner at a restaurant, like ribs. It must have been from when I'd last gone out with Madison. I started to clean myself up, but then realized that was probably not a good idea. I had to go down to the police station and file a report. Legality being new to us, things like hospitals and police stations didn't come as our first instinct like it did for the humans.

So, I stuffed the wasted wipe into the center console and started the engine.

Looking around, I saw that the Whites' car was already gone. For the best, I was sure, in case they decided to follow me so Regina White could be hysterical at me for a little while longer. I took a moment to chastise myself for nasty thoughts, then I pulled out onto the road and made my way back to the center of town.

After the legalization, Adelheid became one of the foremost communities for preternaturals in the entire state of Connecticut, and even in New England. Hell, one could say for the entire United States. Many of the people behind Cameron's Law had chosen to settle here, like I had. At least, those who were still around to tell the tale.

This meant that the streets were busy pretty much all the time. Not even the hours past midnight were safe. I navigated the usual ebbing and flowing of traffic as I made my way downtown.

My shoulder was stiff and sore, because being dead had not taken away the pleasures of either of those things. I felt a twinge as I turned into the parking lot of the Adelheid police station. It was generally busy, like any average business, but I didn't see any uniforms rushing out with riot gear or choppers overhead, so I made the well-educated guess there were no emergencies taking place, and my little assault report could be taken.

I walked up to the front desk, and the eyes of the woman behind it snapped directly to my chest and not for any reason I could be flattered by. "I assume you're here to file a complaint?" she asked, dragging her eyes up to mine.

"That's a very astute observation," I said wryly. "Could you point me in the right direction?"

"Do you need to see a doctor first?"

I knew she was trying to do her job and be a nice person,

so I managed to stop the next words that really wanted to come out of my mouth, which were to point out that if I had needed to see a doctor, I would have already done so. "No, I'm okay." It was sort of true.

She nodded, despite not looking entirely convinced, and gave me directions. I didn't know her name, but it wasn't the first time I had seen her. It wasn't my first time in the station either, since my expertise was sometimes called upon to assist in community-related matters. This was, however, the first time I had come in as a victim. To this station, at least.

Following her directions, I got to the squad room and saw another vaguely familiar person, and she was one you didn't forget. She was pretty enough, but she had scars over the entire left side of her face that looked like someone had finger painted on her. She sat on the edge of the desk belonging to a man whose face I couldn't see because his back was to me.

Even if not a friend, precisely, I naturally gravitated towards familiarity and walked towards that desk. As I neared, the woman looked up and saw me. She nodded. As she did, the man turned his chair. Meeting his eyes caught me off guard and I nearly stumbled. It wasn't really that he was *that* good-looking. I mean, he was attractive, but it was the eyes that got me. They were a shade of brown so light they were almost amber, and there was a raw intensity that drove straight through me like a lightning bolt. As cliched as that sounded.

"Detectives," I greeted, needing to get something said just to pull me away from the man's eyes. In truth, it was amazing anyone could distract from the female detective's face, but there it was.

"Miss Stanton, what brings you..." Her words trailed off as her eyes fell to my bloody shirt. After a moment, she lifted her gaze back up to mine. "I take it that you had some trouble?"

"Yeah, you could say that," I said with a rueful half-smile. Taking the edge of my jacket, I pulled back the lapel to give them a better view of the hole in my shirt and the blood dried all around its ragged edges. The skin directly under it was healed, clear and pale, but there was blood there, too. "Someone tried to stake me, which was all kinds of fun. If I had a name beyond 'psycho bitch,' I would want to file a more specific complaint, of course."

"Indeed," Detective Nykk Marlowe agreed dryly. She waved at the man in the chair. "This is Vance Johnston. He's new here." She looked down at him. "Why don't you cover this one? I've got some paperwork to finish up from the Salinger case."

Johnston looked a little surprised, but he nodded. Marlowe gave me a parting glance before heading off to a different part of the squad room. I took the chair next to his desk without being invited.

"Did you go to the hospital?" he asked. I couldn't tell if it was protocol or concern that prompted the question, but I guessed it was more the former than the latter.

"No point," I replied. "It was healed by the time I would have gotten there."

"Vampire?"

A question that hadn't been commonplace in police stations just a few years ago. I was actually kind of amused by that thought and laughed a little.

He arched a brow at me. "What's so funny?"

"Just life, Detective," I replied.

I sniffed the air then, curious about him. He was a shapeshifter, some kind of cat. I couldn't know what specifically, but I could tell that much. There was peace between all the preternatural species for the sake of keeping the humans from revoking *our* law, but that didn't always mean old prejudices didn't linger. Vampires and shifters in days-gone-by hadn't always been the best of buddies, but I hoped he wouldn't hold my race against me just like I wasn't going to hold his against him.

"Anyways," I went on. "I am indeed a vampire. Hence the staking."

"Right," he said. He shuffled through some papers on his desk and found what I presumed was a statement form or something equally bureaucratic. "Alright, what can you tell me?"

"Besides the obvious?"

Those striking amber eyes lifted to mine, halfway between annoyed and amused. "Yes."

I smiled a little. "Well, I was at St. Gertrude's on a job. Seeing if someone was still in their grave or not." I caught his next look and answered the question before he asked. "Using my senses and not a shovel." He snorted and went back to writing. "It was for Ernest and Regina White. I'd have to call my secretary for the number. Anyway, it was Regina's father. I had done my part and was getting up then, *bam*, out of nowhere, I've got this stick poking out of my chest."

"Did you not hear her coming?" he asked. "I mean. Vampire senses and all."

"They aren't infallible, Detective," I said dryly. "I was focused elsewhere."

He made one of those obnoxious 'hmm' noises that men make when they don't want to commit to any other answer before continuing. "Can you describe her?"

I thought back. "Not much. It happened pretty fast, especially for a human. So, I guess that's the first thing. She was human. About my height? Give or take an inch or two. Blonde, I could see that much. Hair was sort of around shoulder-length...I think. I didn't really see her face. Leather jacket and boots." I thought a little more, but then I had to shrug. "That's all I can tell you."

"We'll see what we can find out," he said when we were finished and I'd signed the thing. "But there's not much to work with."

"It's hardly like I could stop and take a picture," I drawled.

He smiled slightly. "I would expect so." He put the papers to one side, and his eyes held mine for a moment. "You're free to go, Miss Stanton."

There was that 'miss' again.

I was just going to have to make up a title for myself.

Chapter Two

For some reason I couldn't have explained even if asked, I went straight from the station to the office. Any sane person would have gone home first and changed their clothes, but maybe I thought that a little blood would make me look... I don't know, like I had been working hard rather than hardly working? An actual wound had to be a sign of hard work, right?

Madison St John looked up from her computer screen when I walked through the door. At first, she smiled, but then she saw my shirt and sighed. "Oh, Sadie, what happened this time?"

"Hey," I said in my defense, "I don't get my clothing bloody all that often, so don't take that tone with me."

"You get really snappish when you get stabbed, don't you?" she said easily. The werewolf navigated my moods as easily as any sailor on the water. "Why didn't you go home first? I mean, I know we're a small upstart business and all, but I think looking professional probably does mean not having dried blood on your clothing." We exchanged dry expressions. "Oh, there's a lawyer waiting in your office."

My not-beating heart jumped into my throat. "What? What'd I do?"

Madison laughed at my alarm. "He's here to interview," she said. "Relax, Sadie, and just try to pretend you own the place."

"You're just so funny," I muttered and looked down at myself. I didn't have any spare clothes here, and it would take too long to go home while the guy was waiting, so it looked like I was out of luck. Until, that was, Madison handed something across her desk to me.

"I keep a spare for such occasions as pasta sauce at dinner, but being a vampire, blood kind of counts in the same way for you." She smiled.

She really was the little sister I'd never had.

Chuckling, I took the shirt from her and was glad we were just about the same size. "I appreciate it," I said, deciding that I should scale back the attitude with someone who was saving my image. I went into the bathroom and changed. The shirt buttoned up but was a little snug around my chest, giving perhaps a better view of my cleavage than I generally liked, but it seemed an improvement over bloody holes.

Reemerging, I gave her the ruined one to hide behind the desk and got an encouraging smile as I walked into my office, feeling mostly like the boss.

"Hi, I'm sorry to have kept you waiting," I said with my best polite smile as I walked around his chair, stopping to offer my hand, which he shook, before I went the rest of the way to sit. "I'm Sadie Stanton. Madison told me that you're here to interview?"

"Yes, it's a pleasure to meet you, Miss Stanton," he said with a smooth smile and a smoother voice. "My name is Bill Coffen." He held up a hand. "Yes, I know, I've heard all the jokes."

I smiled. "It could be worse," I said. "You could be a vampire."

☾O☽

The interview went well, and it looked like I had found my

demon lawyer.

Mr. Coffen wasn't a demon himself, but he was versed in human law as well as multi-dimensional law. "Demons," in our community, were just from other dimensions, and you could call on them to make deals for things you couldn't manage to get done on your own in the real world. It required a summoner, of course, but it also required a lawyer to make the deal because they could be very tricky things.

After he'd left, I got to work. Doing administrative work is, of course, as glamorous as it sounds.

When the workday was done, I was, too.

"Alright, I'm heading home," I said to Madison as I trudged into the front office. "I'll see you there."

"I will probably be late because I have some paperwork to finish. Mind stopping at the butcher for me?" she asked, looking up from the stacks of stuff upon stuff that existed on her desk like a paper village in the making.

"Sure," I said. "The usual."

"Yep."

I tossed off a casual salute and headed out the door, into my car, and down the street.

Most businesses these days were open almost all the time, but the butcher especially because they were the only "grocery store" a vampire could use. Supplies of blood that would have been wasted in the before-days were now in hot demand.

There were already a few customers inside Adelheid's butcher shop. I passed another vampire coming out as I was going in. I didn't know their name offhand, though I had seen them around, so we did the cursory polite neighborhood smile before going about our business. Which, in this case, was waiting in line.

Once it was my turn at the counter, the gaze of the man in the white coat on the other side snapped down to my somewhat-bursting shirt buttons. At least this time, I knew it was a reason I could be flattered by. I didn't know him and hadn't seen him here before, so I chose not to say anything and bust on him about it. I just waited patiently, smirking, until he met my eyes and asked what he could help me with.

"Yeah, I need some ribeyes and some chicken," I said, starting to list off my werewolf roommate's usual carnivorous order.

He nodded. "We can do that. Any blood for yourself today?"

I tilted my head and inhaled quickly. Ah. Shifter. He could tell what I was. "No, not today."

"Are you sure, ma'am?" he asked as he packaged things from the selection in the cooler counter. "It's never good to run out."

I wasn't ever happy with the hard-sell, so I just put on a more serious look and shook my head. "No. I'm good. Thank you."

For a moment, it looked like he was going to say something more, but then he stopped himself and went about wrapping the things I had actually asked for. I took the package, enjoying the smell of things I could no longer eat, and paid the bill before heading out.

❨O❩

Home was a small two-bedroom house on Maple Street, which was about five minutes from the agency. Looking at the skyline, my body easily sensed I only had a couple more hours before I needed to go to 'bed' and sleep through the daylight hours. In the darkness, my vampire sight could tell that the lawn needed mowing, and I hoped Madison might take care of it when there was light out. I didn't trust myself with the lawn mower, and some of my neighbors were non-vampires who wouldn't appreciate the noise at that hour, anyway.

I dropped the files I'd brought home with me on the coffee table, put the meat in the fridge, grabbed myself a snack, and then went straight for the bedroom to change into more comfortable clothing before settling down on the couch to read resumes.

One of the positions I was looking to fill was for a hunter. They would fill the traditional bounty hunter role, tracking down bail jumpers who happened to be preternatural, but also would work on hunting down any supernatural being the police didn't feel they were able to take care of.

A good hunter was hard to find, but I wanted to find one to work out of my office. This person might also take on private cases, but always with the permission of the police so they wouldn't be arrested for kidnapping or murder if things got messy.

Unfortunately, the job tended to attract...well, psychopaths was the best word for them. You could only tell so much from a resume, yet I didn't take keenly to the idea of inviting psychopaths into my office. It's one thing when it is walk-in crazy, but inviting it in on purpose is another matter entirely.

Still, I didn't see any way around it, so I culled through the resumes as best as I was able and checked the call times. I required that every applicant place what times they were available for calls in their cover letters or on their resumes. Obviously, as a vampire, it was important for me to know I could call them during the night and it wouldn't be a problem. Otherwise, we'd never speak.

First, I ruled out anyone who couldn't follow simple directions and didn't put their call times anywhere. Second, I ruled out anyone with the wrong call times. Why people thought they wouldn't work nights at a preternatural gig was beyond me. I shuffled out a few who didn't have enough experience, or the kind I was looking for.

I had more applications for this spot than any other, and I was pretty sure it went back to the psychopath theory. In the end, I was left with three applications, and I made calls. Two ended in voicemail, and the third I got in person, so I scheduled an appointment with that one and would just have to wait on the others.

I was just putting the folders on the coffee table when Madison walked in.

"You can't be serious," she declared, dropping her purse on the floor and all but throwing herself onto the couch beside me. "You work all night, get stabbed, work some more, then come home and work even more?" She took the folders and smacked me on the head. "You're nuts!"

"No," I muttered, snatching the folders away. "I'm busy. There's a difference."

"There is, and I say you're nuts." She tore the folders from my hands and threw them on the table. "You need to start having a life, Sadie."

I sighed and was briefly tempted to grab them back, if for no reason other than to make a point, but I resisted the urge. "I'm a vampire. I don't have life."

Her expression told me she wasn't at all impressed. "You can be as many kinds of sarcastic as you want, but I don't care. All you do is work, and that's not healthy, even for a vampire. Not that I think a vampire should just lounge around like a satin-covered second base, but still, there needs to be some balance."

Sinking down against the cushion, I just wanted to melt into it and get away from her. The hardest part of it was I knew she was right, but that didn't mean I wanted to admit it.

"Do you know how tired I get of hearing this?" I asked.

"I hope so." She leaned into the cushions beside me and

put her head on my shoulder like a little sister, which she kind of was. "Maybe if you get tired enough, then you'll do something about it, and I won't have to say it anymore."

I leaned my head against hers. "I could just kill you."

She jabbed her elbow into my side. "You know you'd never hurt me," she said with well-placed confidence. "Besides, I'm right. And I think you know it. I could pull out the big guns, but I imagine you wouldn't appreciate it."

"You imagine right," I murmured. I really didn't need her playing *that* card on me.

She sort of did anyway. "You still miss him, don't you?" Madison's voice was soft now.

I nodded. "Every day," I said. "I never realized just how bloody attached to him I'd gotten until..."

"Yeah," she supplied, not forcing me to finish the statement. "I miss him, too. He was a really good big brother, and it's hard to live all your life with him watching out for you and then suddenly not have him anymore. I just always remember that he wouldn't want me wallowing over him forever. He'd want me to live." She looked up at me. "And he'd want you to do the same thing." Another nudge to my ribs. "Even if it's not life like the rest of us."

"Fine, fine," I muttered. "But not right now. I can feel dawn coming on, and I need to get to my room." Shrugging one shoulder, I pushed her off. "See you at dusk, Madison, and try not to get into any trouble." I stuck my tongue out at her as I got to my feet and went down the hall to my little bedroom.

I checked the black-out curtains on the single window to make sure they were fully covering the glass. The last thing I needed was to have a careless beam of sun drop onto my bed and fry me while I was dead to the world.

CHAPTER THREE

I woke with a gasp. It was the same way every night, so I had stopped thinking about why that was a long time ago.

Madison was gone by the time I wandered out into the rest of the house, but that was pretty usual. She'd be in the office soon to catch up on messages and get started on the night's business. As much as we teased and bugged each other, I couldn't run the business without her.

It was a standard evening. I showered and dressed, had breakfast, and checked to see if I had any messages. After that, I ran a few errands, which were ultimately all very banal. Just like all the other myths, being a vampire did not automatically make your life exciting or glamorous, and you didn't come equipped with servants. Vampires still had to do things like go to the bank, buy food, and do their laundry.

Once I was done with the errands, I headed to the office. I had the radio on, which switched over to the news as I made my turn.

"In Adelheid, around dawn this morning, a vampire attacked a werewolf in front of the bus stop on the corner of South and Walters. Information is limited, and police aren't commenting at this time, but we've heard from a witness that there was no provocation, and the vampire did not attempt to feed…"

I drowned out the voice as she moved onto another topic, but what I'd heard was enough to make me want to throw up, if my body had still been capable of it.

This…was not good.

It wasn't good for the werewolf who was attacked, of course, but at least they hadn't said it was a fatality. Worse than that, our entire community was still fighting like hell to prove we weren't monsters. This was a community disaster as well.

When I walked in, Madison looked up. Her expression was rueful. "I can tell from your look that you heard," she said. It was like she was psychic sometimes. It really was.

"I did," I confirmed, tossing my bag down on the waiting room sofa. "Do you know anything more than the radio?" I hoped she did because it would certainly help me out, but I also hoped she didn't because that would make it more real, and I didn't feel like dealing with it.

"A female werewolf, a college student, was coming home from an all-night party, like college students do, right? I heard all this from a friend of mine who's in the pack, and he heard it through the wolf vine. Anyways, she's waiting on the corner for the bus to take her home when a vampire, another chick, just comes out of nowhere and grabs her and just goes at her. She's biting without trying to feed, just tearing and clawing. The wolf fights her off and shouts for help. A couple people come running up and try to wrestle the vamp off. They manage it but get a little knocked around in the process. No serious injuries for them, and hers have been healing pretty well so she's not in danger. Vamp ran away into the night and parts unknown."

I pinched the bridge of my nose. "Were the rescuers humans?"

Pause. "Yes."

Great, now monsters were fighting in the street and hurting humans in the process.

"You say they're all okay, though?" I asked, still squeezing one eye shut.

"Yes." Madison nodded. "The wolf is in the hospital, but she'll be okay. I hear that she's managed to make a sketch of the vamp to see if anyone knows who it is. I haven't heard if they've heard anything yet or found anyone."

I rubbed my temples as I thought it over. It happened near dawn, which meant it wasn't a young vampire. The more a vampire ages, the closer to dawn and dusk they are able to stay awake. The young ones often run at the first molecule.

But that being the case, this could not be explained by youthful frenzy.

Becoming a vampire means getting a lot of power very suddenly, and most of us have mentors to help us learn to control it. The older we get, the easier we can control ourselves but, sometimes, the young ones lose it, especially if there's no one watching them. The timing, however, ruled out youth.

That was a frightening thought.

"We've already gotten a few calls," she added after a moment.

I closed my eyes, even though I knew it was futile. I had suddenly gone from being almost a hundred to being five. I was that little kid who stands in the middle of the room with their hands over their eyes, shouting, "You can't see me!"

"Why are they calling us?" I asked, but I already knew the answer. "Ignore that question and just tell me who."

"You're not going to like it."

I squeezed my eyes shut even tighter and weighed the usefulness of putting my hands over my ears and singing *Camptown Races*.

"Linda Smith." She nodded. I couldn't see it, but I just knew. "Which means you should just stake me now." I put my hand over my chest. "Right here, just get it over with."

"Next time she calls, I could just tell her that you're dead," she offered. "After all, it would be the truth." Somehow,

I heard her grin.

Finally, I opened my eyes, but only because I wanted to give her a dry look. "I'm really tempted to tell you to try it, but I doubt it would work."

Madison chuckled. "She is a persistent bitch, isn't she?"

That was the nice way of putting it.

Linda Smith was the leader of an organization known as LOHAV. They were the League of Humans against Vampires, although they hated all preternatural species equally. It hadn't taken long for the group to come together when the legislation began for Cameron's Law, also known as the Preternatural Civil Rights Act of 2010. There were other groups, but LOHAV was the biggest and loudest and meanest. They were the ones most likely to engage in back-alley politics where intimidation and even physical assaults were not unheard of, and some were even fatal.

I really, really hated that woman.

"Is she the only one who's called?" I didn't really want the answer.

"There were a couple of reporters, but I played the evasion game with them, too," she said.

"Why don't you just hang up with a nice curt 'no comment'?"

She smiled, stretched, and got to her feet. "Because I like fucking with them." She was shameless.

I wished I could shrug things off as easily as she did. I knew she carried some stuff pretty deep inside, but a lot of it she let roll off her back. That was something I envied about her. "Is there anything else I need to know about? Stuff that perhaps actually pertains to our jobs?"

"Not really," Madison replied. "You had some appointments confirmed and calls returned." She handed me a few slips of paper. Despite being so much younger, she could be as old-fashioned as I was. I liked that. Or maybe she just did it for me. Either way, I appreciated it.

Taking the papers, I got up and took my bag. "Thanks," I said as I passed her desk and went to my office. "Oh, and if Smith calls again," I called over my shoulder, "tell her I'm dead."

☽ ◯ ☾

Over the past two years, I had learned a very important lesson: politics and public relations meant a lot of phone calls. Never in more than nine decades had I ever spent so much time on the phone as I had since the process of Cameron's Law began, and it hadn't stopped since. If only it would, because it was exhausting.

Tonight really wasn't any different. The community had all heard by now, and they were all concerned. Nothing could bring people together like terror.

My first call, however, was to Jade.

Jade was the only name I knew for her. She was the leader of Adelheid's vampire coven, of which I had chosen not to join but still remained closely allied with. She was the one the police would go to first with that sketch, and I figured I had a better chance of getting her to talk to me than the cops.

Her personal assistant answered, but I was connected right away.

"Sadie," she greeted. Her voice was, as ever, elegant and cultured. I'd never heard her sound otherwise.

"Hello, Jade."

"You've heard?"

"Of course."

"This is quite terrible." The elder vampire sighed. I didn't really know how old she was, but it was over five hundred. She had power.

"It definitely is. Have the police been to see you?" I didn't waste time getting right to the point, because I knew that was what she preferred.

"Yes. They showed me a sketch."

"Did you know her?"

"She was not a coven vampire."

I rolled my eyes, grateful she couldn't see me. "Neither am I, but you still know me. You didn't answer the question."

There was a faint trace of amusement in her voice. "No. I did not know her. Honestly, I wish that I did. It would make all of this conclude much quicker."

"Indeed it would." I sighed. "Indeed it would."

Chapter Four

After I finished my call with Jade, I had an interview with a summoner. It went well enough, but my mind was elsewhere.

"I hope you haven't forgotten that you have other appointments tonight," Madison said as she leaned her head into my office.

"Of course not." But I kicked myself internally as I got up and started getting my things together. I paused and looked at her with a sheepish expression. "And what appointments were those again?"

Madison's expression told me she had known I'd been lying, so she didn't have to say anything else. "It was an appointment made at the last moment from some woman that thinks she has a preternatural critter in her house."

Oh, that sounded promising. "What makes her think this?" It wasn't like it would have been the first prank call I'd ever gotten, if it was a prank. I kind of hoped it was, because I hated chasing out preternatural critters.

What, you may ask, is a preternatural critter? Well, like not-preternatural creatures, they come in all forms and shapes and sizes. Usually, they're regular creatures that have somehow ended up with generally harmless but endlessly annoying bits of magic. Some are fae creatures that look like tiny people but act like bipedal animals. The worst case I ever had was a shifter trapped in animal form, where its mind had reverted to the primal. It was basically like a giant feral dog that had three times as much power as your average animal.

"She says it eats her food," Madison said, "And doesn't bother to close cabinet or fridge doors when it's done."

"Any teenagers in the house?" This seemed like the next logical question.

Madison shook her head. "No hungry, forgetful husbands either." She answered my next question before I even had the chance to ask it.

I sighed. "Does the city have its preternatural animal control running yet?"

"Nope."

"Is there any way I can professionally and responsibly get out of this?"

"Nope."

"Fine," I muttered, "but I'm not looking forward to it."

With my bag over my shoulder, I headed for the door. Madison smiled at me on my way by. "I don't care if you're happy. Mama's got bills to pay."

I didn't bother replying and, instead, waited until she gave me the address. I headed for my car and was on my way. Conversely, I wasn't sure whether I was hoping for a supernatural mongrel or not. If it wasn't, it would be easier to get rid of. If it was, I wouldn't have wasted the trip and the client's money. Not that I minded taking money, but no one liked to feel like they'd wasted it. And maybe irrationally resent me for it 'cause I'm not psychic.

Just at the edge of town, I pulled up in front of a farmhouse that looked like it had been built sometime around the town's founding in 1897, but it was nicely maintained. Being this far out in the woods, I wasn't surprised there was some kind of animal problem.

Grabbing my bag, I walked to the door and knocked. For some reason, I had the thought flash through my head that there might be a bleach-blonde with a stake behind the door, even though that was ridiculous. I hoped it was, at least, and was relieved when a middle-aged redhead answered without a stake in sight.

"I'm Sadie Stanton." I pulled my card out of my pocket to hand to her. "You called us about a possible supernatural infestation?"

"Yes," she replied, her uncertain expression lightening with relief. "Thank you for coming on such short notice." She invited me in and talked while she led me up to the second story. In the hallway, I learned she lived alone. By the stairs, I knew her husband had passed away two years before, and she'd had trouble staying on top of the upkeep.

"My secretary told me that you've been hearing noises at night and have had food eaten from your kitchen?" I asked, trying to gently steer her around to my reason for coming. I could tell she needed to talk, and I wasn't usually the type to be unkind, but I did have a schedule to keep.

She didn't seem to take it badly, though, as she nodded. "That's about the size of it," she agreed. "Cabinets get left open, and even the fridge from time to time. I'd been hearing in the news that there were some infestations of those wild-like fae creatures, and I wondered if I might have some of them hiding in my attic."

The way up to the attic was a flight of old stairs that scared me a little and led up to a door with a broken lock. Vampire, creature of the night that I was, stood staring up those stairs, wondering if some dude with a hook for a hand was waiting for me.

"I'll go check it out," I said with far more confidence than I felt as I began my ascent.

Things started off better than I expected when I actually made it up the stairs without falling through any of them like some suspenseful bridge-crossing scene in an action-adventure movie. At the top, I carefully opened the door and leaned in to see if there was a light of some kind.

"There's a flashlight on the floor to your right," the lady called up after me.

Now, vampires do have very good night vision, but it's not always perfect. Absolute darkness is still tough for us to see in, and this was absolute darkness. There were no windows of any kind. I reached down to pick up the flashlight. Any good points scored for making it up the stairs crashed right back down again with that.

Shining the pale beam ahead of me, I stepped into the darkness and felt a twinge of anxiety slipping along my spine. It wasn't that I didn't think I could handle whatever was up here, but it was more the fear of being startled. Like the way people are afraid of mice. You're not really afraid of that tiny fuzzy beast, but you're afraid of it startling you. I shone the light around, searching for my metaphorical squeaker.

After a moment, I stopped walking. It was perfect silence, because I didn't need to breathe and had no pulse to pound in my ears. I listened and it was faint, but I heard a heartbeat. It was something small. At least, smaller than a human. That meant it wasn't some kind of vampire creature, and I got the feeling that it wasn't a shifter of any kind. I couldn't exactly explain how I could tell, but I had the experience.

That still left several possibilities, and I moved forward cautiously, wishing that I'd hired a hunter by now or that Adelheid had gotten its act together for a preternatural animal control, so I didn't have to do this shit.

It took a little while, although I wasn't paying attention to how long, but then I heard the very faint scratching sound of small claws on wood, and when I paid very close attention, I could hear a furry body sliding along the wall. So, it wasn't a fae. It was small and it had fur.

My senses were working overtime with my concentration which, sadly, was heightened with that fear of being startled. I felt it like a little twitch in my shoulders. No, I don't know how a creature that technically doesn't have any nerve impulses firing feels these things, but there it was.

I started bravely—I thought so, at least—moving towards the back left corner where I heard the noises. The attic was so musty I couldn't really pick up the scent of anything else and was just going to have to wait till I found it.

Suddenly, the flashlight illuminated two spots and a dark little nose from the shadows, and I hopped back a step until I realized what I had done and felt very embarrassed, despite the fact that no one had seen me. I swallowed my not-pounding heart back down from my throat and focused on what I saw.

I realized I was looking straight into the eyes of a terrifying...raccoon.

He looked just as annoyed at my presence as I was at his.

"Dude, you can just hang out for a while. I'm not qualified to handle your kind," I told him, and then turned right around, went downstairs, and gave the homeowner the number to the *real* animal control. "It's just a raccoon. They are very clever creatures and can open cabinets, so I can at least assure you that there's nothing supernatural up there. Just call that number and they'll take care of it. No charge for my visit."

She seemed as embarrassed about the matter as I had been about being startled by the stupid thing and as the raccoon was about being caught, so all three of us slunk back about our business.

❪O❫

The next appointment I went to was the sort that I would usually want people to come into the office for and save me the driving, but she was home-bound so I made an exception. She was human, but I'd known her on and off for some years.

Driving along on the streets, I got a strange tingling feeling on the back of my neck every time I looked in my rear-view. It was a mouse feeling. It had something to do with a set of headlights I saw, which seemed to stick with me. Was I being followed? It seemed like something to consider with the same car behind me for so long, but I couldn't imagine why anyone would follow *me*.

I figured the only logical conclusion was that I was crazy. I ignored it. After all, it wasn't unusual for people to be driving around town so late.

By the time I reached my client's home, I had mostly managed to shake it off and walk up to the door feeling like myself again. I also just barely escaped the stake-wielding images that hit me at the last door I walked up to. I knocked.

Fran Warren answered the door a few moments later. She was a woman in her fifties with various health conditions that made it hard for her to leave her house. Smiling warmly, she greeted me and invited me into her living room. Moving laboriously, she walked down the hall, and we both sat.

"What can I do for you?" I asked after we'd settled in and exchanged the usual pleasantries.

"It's about my brother," she began. "I don't know if you remember him. His name is Walter. Anyways, I haven't heard from him in several days, and I'm getting worried."

I frowned. "Why did you call me and not the police?" It seemed like a logical question, right?

She smiled ruefully. "I did. I called you both. The reason that I called you as well was that I think he might have been turned and has been avoiding me."

I didn't ask why he would have needed to avoid her because of that and figured that she couldn't have too big a problem with vampires since I sat here in her house, so instead, I went to the next logical question. "Why do you think he may have been turned?"

"I don't really know," she said. "I guess it's just a feeling. I just remember him talking about vampires a lot before he stopped calling, and I couldn't reach him anymore."

"What kind of things?"

She shook her head. "I don't remember exactly. It's just an impression left on my mind that I keep coming back to." Frowning, she paused. "Do you know how it is when, say, you've seen a movie that wasn't too good but wasn't too bad? You don't remember what happened, just a general idea. That's how I feel about the conversations we had. I remember big concepts from them but not the details."

I nodded, because I understood her point. She had described it very well. "Vampires can be notoriously hard to find when they don't wish to be," I pointed out, "but I'll look into it and see what I can do. It would help if you told me a little more about your brother."

Over the next fifteen minutes, I learned his name was Walter Warren and he was fifty-seven years old. He had a PhD, was a microbiologist doing "something in medicine," though she didn't know what exactly, and he didn't have much of a social life. He had become more reclusive after his wife left him several months before, for a man that Fran didn't know much about. I got an address, phone number, and a workplace, though she had already called his house, his cell phone, and his work with no luck. She'd had one of his co-workers check his house, which was dark and locked up.

I had one thing I could try that a human couldn't, but I didn't want to freak her out so I didn't mention it.

Having gathered what information I could, I made some more assurances that I would see what I could find out, and then I left. I drove away from her house and parked in front of a nearby gas station to make a few phone calls, but all the calls I made had the same result. I moved onto the address she'd given me, which was only about ten minutes away.

There wasn't a car in the driveway, and the house was dark and locked, just as had been reported. I looked around to see if there was anyone to call the police on me for loitering and, seeing the coast was apparently clear, I walked the perimeter as close to the house as possible. I smelled and listened and looked through windows, being a very skilled stalker, but the curtains were all drawn so I couldn't see anything.

I do not, after all, have x-ray vision.

But I didn't smell anything either. There wasn't a dead body in there, or any blood having been spilled. There were no heartbeats anywhere that I could tell, and since it was a one-story house, I didn't have to worry about a second floor.

By all accounts and senses, he wasn't there.

CHAPTER FIVE

There were more cars than I had expected parked in front of my building, and since the lot wasn't very big in the first place, and someone in a blue SUV had parked in my spot despite the sign marking it as mine, I had to park on the street. That pretty much knocked my mood down several flights of stairs before I even walked in the door, and once I'd done that, there was nothing to bring it up again.

On the small television in my front office, standing at a podium, puffed up like he was the very Voice of God himself, was Frederick Hughes, face flushed with righteous fury: the man who had spent all of his time and energy making my life a living hell during the legality trials. He'd worked just as hard to be a headache to every preternatural in existence since he didn't win, the big-city lawyer who used his time and knowledge to keep us down, rather than try to better society. He thought keeping us down was bettering society.

"You should have listened to me one year ago when I said that nothing good would come of this!" He pounded his fist on the podium. "These creatures of the night, these demons, are now viscously attacking each other and endangering the life of every human around them! These are not people. They are nothing more than animals and should be treated as such."

I was too busy standing in my doorway, staring dumbfounded at the television, to realize there was a client in the room. At least, not until she was on her feet and shouting at the television, acting out what I was doing in my head.

"You moron! Like humans aren't constantly attacking humans and endangering *us* even more often!"

"Let's just take a deep breath, everyone," I said, trying to be the voice of reason as I shut the door behind me. Madison was sitting behind her desk and had put all of her usual vivacity in a drawer. I understood why. "We all know the man is an idiot, and I'll bet he's been one since the day he was born. You can't learn stupid like that. It's got to be genetic. He tried to keep us from being legal a year ago and he failed. He's not going to hurt us now."

Madison didn't say anything, but she did meet my eye. The other woman turned to face me with an embarrassed expression, although her cheeks were still flushed with anger. I smelled dog and recognized her for a shifter with a canine form. Coyote, maybe. It was hard to tell.

She offered her hand. "I'm sorry, but the man is so aggravating," she apologized as we shook.

"You don't have to explain yourself to me," I replied. "Believe me, I completely understand, but we can't let him get to us." Look at me, sounding all grown up.

We exchanged introductions before being interrupted by another fist-pounding declaration from the television. "These beasts can't even control themselves," he shouted over the applause of the mindless. "Vampires attacking werewolves in the street! This is not real life but cinema. Why have we let these creatures walk free on our streets?" There was more applause, and I felt the collective blood pressure of the room rising.

Crossing the space quickly, I turned the television off. "No one needs to watch that shit." Both women looked grateful, like they'd wanted to but couldn't manage it on their own. Pausing there, I sighed. "I'd like to know where he's getting his information." Perhaps it would have been smarter to move off the subject of Hughes entirely, but I didn't really see how that was possible.

"I wouldn't be surprised if the cops have a few members of LOHAV hiding in their ranks," Madison said quietly.

"It wouldn't surprise me either," I sighed, "but it bothers the hell out of me. The cops are supposed to protect us, too." I looked at the dark television for a moment, imagining Hughes getting redder in the face as his stupid speech really ramped up, and then turned to Madison. "Has the press started calling yet?"

"Just one," she replied. She handed me a slip of paper.

Taking it, I took one glance down at the name, crumpled it up, and tossed it in the trash. "No further word from Linda Smith?"

Madison shook her head. "Not yet," she said, "but I'm sure it's only a matter of time."

I headed for my office, but then stopped. Frowning, I glanced back at the client who sat in one of the waiting chairs. "Do I have an appointment?" I asked.

"No," Madison replied, "she's here to fill out some paperwork, and we got distracted by the television."

"Oh." I nodded. "All right, well, good then. If Smith calls, you know what to tell her."

Madison smirked in an uncharacteristically dark way. "Yeah, I know what to tell her."

I paused next to her desk and looked at her with concern. "Are you okay?"

She looked up with a sad smile. "I'll be all right. I just really hate it when all this shit gets stirred up again, you know?"

I smiled sympathetically. "Yeah, I know," I said, and I did. "We just have to hang in there, yeah?"

"Yeah," she agreed. "Besides, we play our cards right, and we'll live longer than he will, anyways." She chuckled, but I could tell it was forced. Still, there wasn't really anything else I could do.

I couldn't make someone be less of a bigot, or an idiot.

☾O☽

I spent the next hour doing whatever tedious busywork I could find that would keep my mind off what I'd seen on television and all the potential repercussions of it.

There was a knock on my door, and I looked up to see Madison. If anyone ever knocked that wasn't her, I was going to be in for a hell of a shock. Thankfully, that day wasn't today because I didn't think my non-beating heart could handle it.

"Detective Johnston is here to see you," she announced, and I could see she had gotten much of her usual good humor back. It wasn't anything specific that she did, I just knew her well enough to tell. Her eyes lit up when she said his name.

Her news surprised me, though. I wondered what he was doing here, and some part of my brain laughingly hoped it wasn't to arrest me for something. "Send him in," I told her as I started sorting out the crap on top of my desk into something that resembled order. When I was done, I didn't see any order at all.

Johnston walked in, looking like...well, looking like a cop. Any moment, I expected to hear some dramatic noise like from a detective show.

"Have a seat." I waved my hand invitingly at the chairs before my desk while Madison silently slipped out and shut the door. We both sat because I'd stood at some point I hadn't remembered. "What can I do for you?" I was very curious.

"Well, I've already been to see Jade with this," he said, holding up a folder. "She didn't recognize the face, so I thought that maybe you would."

"If Jade doesn't, I'm not likely to," I admitted ruefully.

"She knows more of the vampires in this city. If I didn't know better, I'd think you were looking for an excuse to see me, Detective."

He shrugged what I now noticed to be impressively broad shoulders, looking almost sheepish. "It doesn't hurt to check, right?"

I nodded, and he handed the folder to me. I opened it to see an unhappy woman's face looking back at me, and I wondered if she always looked like that or if it was just because that was how she'd been when the wolf saw her. I studied the face for several moments, but then I shook my head and handed it back.

"I'm sorry. I don't know her."

He nodded and then got to his feet. "Well, thank you anyway, Miss Stanton."

'Miss' again... "Call me Sadie," I said with a smile.

He paused and smiled. It was a really nice smile. "Call me Vance." He paused again. "Do you, uh, go out for coffee?"

My brows rose. "Well, I can meet someone at a coffee shop and talk."

Vance chuckled. "Would you like to do that with me some time?"

I smiled again. "Sure."

CHAPTER SIX

After that, it was back to work. I had another interview for a summoner, a kid named Donovan, who was so talented it was a little scary. After that, more phone calls, and more paperwork, and more…I don't even know. All the stuff that goes into the behind-the-scenes of owning your own business is really just mind-blurring tedium.

"Here's the mail," Madison said, popping into my office for the sixteenth or seventeenth time that night. This time, she tossed a stack of envelopes on my desk.

Her being her, I knew she would have taken out all the bills because she handled the accounting, but as payback for that, she left me with all the junk mail and flyers. I started sorting through them, and anything that was a single sheet of card stock with bright colors on it got automatically tossed into the recycling bin because I didn't need 20% off car detailing and couldn't care less that tomatoes were on sale at the grocery store.

Halfway through the stack, I found a plain white envelope. It was bigger than a regular one but smaller than a sheet-size mailer. I frowned and wondered what it was. It was addressed directly to me, but there wasn't a return address. Postmark said it was mailed from right here in southeast CT.

I tore open the top seam with my fingernail and carefully pulled out what was inside. It turned out to be an equally boring piece of white paper, but written on it, in red ink and block lettering, were the words:

We belong in the shadows.

Now, I was used to getting all sorts of hate mail, and even death threats. They were often creatively worded and designed, as well as factually inaccurate, but this was something else. It was simple, it was grammatically correct, and it wasn't apparently from a human. The use of the word 'we' suggested it was from a preternatural.

I knew there were those of us out there that hated being what we were, but I usually didn't get mail from them. They generally just kept hiding away, or "passing" for a regular mortal.

I dropped it a bit like it was on fire, which it rather felt like it was.

"Madison," I called.

She popped in a moment later, looking rather cheerful until she saw my face. "What's wrong?"

I just pointed at the paper. She picked it up and frowned.

"Well..." she said, "that's weird."

"It is," I agreed. "It's unnerving."

She walked around my desk and dropped it in the trash. "It's garbage is what it is. Try not to think about it."

That made me do one of those snort-laugh things. "Good luck with that."

She flashed me a smile. "I'm serious. We work to ignore the human idiots. The supernatural population is certainly not immune to its own fools, so we need to ignore them too."

"Right, right," I agreed with her.

"I know I am," she declared as she walked back out.

☾O☽

When the work was done, I decided to go home. As usual, it was before Madison did, but I knew she wouldn't be far behind.

I was still feeling kind of rattled after that letter, so I couldn't say I was surprised when I had that heeby-jeeby feeling that someone was watching me when I walked out into the parking lot. I stood behind my car and looked around, slowly and thoroughly, but I didn't see anyone.

The only heartbeat seemed to be Madison's just behind me.

I sighed, chastised myself for paranoia, and went home.

《O》

If I thought that I would wake up the next night to discover it had all been a dream, I was going to be sorely disappointed.

A vampire had attacked a werewolf and started a disheartening chain of events.

The following night just made it worse.

"Have you heard?" Madison asked the moment I came through the door. I had barely even stepped over the threshold and paused so suddenly that I nearly fell on my face.

I blinked. "Heard what?"

"There's been another attack." She grimaced. I turned and walked right back out the door...

...but came back in a moment later.

"What was it like this time?"

"Vampire guy. Werewolf guy. Near dawn. Ambush. No feeding."

"So, second verse the same as the first?"

"Basically."

I sighed heavily and walked to my office door. "I quit."

After having decided to stick around for a while after all, I settled in to work. I know I would have to call Jade and Gabriel, leader of the Adelheid pack, at some point, but neither were calls I looked forward to. Since they weren't calling me either, I guessed I wasn't the only one who felt that way.

A short time later, Madison popped her head in. "Detective Johnston is here to see you again," she said lightly. "Detective Marlowe as well."

Okay. This was interesting. "Send them in."

They both walked in and stood in front of my desk like they were reporting for duty. I eyed them both for a moment then asked, "What can I do for you?"

"We were hoping that you could help us with something," Marlowe was the first one to speak. She didn't have to make any particular expression, but the terrible scarring on her face made her eyes stand out and her expression perpetually grim. "We would like to speak with Jade more in depth about these recent attacks and see if she knows anything."

Johnston jumped in. "We know we could just flash our shiny badges and get the door to open, but she's sounding...a little more guarded now after this second attack. So, we thought she might be more comfortable, and more receptive, if you could act as a sort of goodwill ambassador between us." He smiled that crooked smile.

"I'm sure Jade is feeling a little gun-shy right now," I said carefully. I didn't want to walk myself into any corners I couldn't get back out of. "She knows this doesn't reflect well on the coven, or the rest of us."

"We understand that," Marlowe said, "which is why we were hoping that you could help us. If you could perhaps arrange the meeting, and give us your...endorsement, we know she would trust you more easily than she would trust us."

I wasn't really sure how Jade felt right now, but I could make some educated guesses. I couldn't see her stonewalling the police, but she might let her guard down a little more if I was there with them.

"Sure. I'll call her and set something up," I finally said. "I can't make any promises she'll be that much more comfortable just because I'm there, but I'll be there."

"That's all we ask," Johnston said, still smiling. "Thank you."

"Of course," I replied. "I want this to be solved as much as you do."

CHAPTER SEVEN

"Explain this to me."

"I already told you that I can't."

I kept going as though she hadn't said anything and entirely ignored her tired tone that bordered on annoyed. "You apply for a job and submit your resume. You go through all that trouble, and then do a follow-up and schedule an appointment. In the act of applying for the job, one presumes that you need the work, right?"

She sighed and kept typing. "Right."

"So, you need the work, and you go through all that trouble, and then you just don't show up or call. How does that work?"

"I haven't yet managed to find the answer I lacked fifteen minutes ago, Sadie."

"You're not being very sympathetic, you know," I muttered. I was sitting on the couch because I had nothing else to do. I had already called Jade and set up the appointment and done whatever paperwork was on my desk before getting ready for the animator appointment that I had set up...

...for someone who wasn't showing.

I knew I had to wait at least a certain amount of time, for propriety's sake, before writing the whole thing off, but that left me with nothing to do but bother Madison. That, I can safely say, I was doing very well.

She stopped typing and finally looked at me. "I *was* sympathetic," she said. "Fifteen minutes ago."

I made a face at her that wasn't really worthy of my age but suited my mood. "I suppose it's been long enough now to write this off?"

"Yes," she agreed emphatically.

Pushing myself up from the couch, I held up my hands in surrender. "Fine, fine." I walked into my office. "I will leave you alone now." As I shut the door behind me, I heard her 'thank you' and then it clicked shut.

Just when I had finally gotten involved with some documents on my computer, Madison stuck her head in. I looked up. "The knocking thing really is just a crapshoot, isn't it?" I asked dryly.

She was smirking. "There is someone here to see you."

"My appointment?" I perked up and yet was also annoyed. They were late. I had already moved on.

"Nope." She shook her head. "It's a walk-in for the same job, and I figured it was okay, since I know you don't have anything else to do. I mean, it's not like you're trying to run a business or anything here."

I snorted. "Clearly, you need more to do. Well, why not? Go ahead and send them in."

There was something about her demeanor that I found suspicious, but maybe I was just over-reading the look in her eyes. At least, I hoped I was. It took only one moment as the walk-in appointment woman swept into my office to understand that it had been mischief I had seen, and I was going to have to hurt Madison later.

"I am Madame Dmitri!" the woman declared theatrically with a wave of her hand. She was dressed in total flower child regalia like a character actor from a gaudy film about the sixties, with so much make-up and loose frizzy hair that I couldn't even begin to guess what her age was. In fact, I wasn't even going to try because I didn't want to know. This book I was damn well judging by the cover.

"Madam—" I got most of that word out before the woman interrupted me, which I didn't think was good protocol for a job interview but since this was blown the moment she walked in the door, did it really matter?

Another flourish of her hand. "I am Madam Dmitri!" she repeated, because clearly my super-hearing hadn't picked up that loud stage voice the first time. "Many a generation have the women in my family been able to raise the dead!" Now that she had said more words, I could hear the terrible accent. If only she knew that I knew *real* people from the regions whose accent she was thieving. She was going for *Dracula* Eastern European. She was achieving carnival ringmaster. "I have a great and terrible power that you will want to make use of and pay me well for."

Wow, that was quick. We were already paying her lots of money to embarrass the reputation we were trying to build. I opened my mouth to speak and was again interrupted.

"I have great power, and you would be foolish to let it go to waste. You must hire me, because the dead will it!"

"Thank you!" I all but shouted, hoping that it would make her finally shut up. I was on my feet in an instant and politely ushering her out. "Thank you for coming in. I will certainly keep this in mind and be in touch soon." I didn't give her a chance to say anything else, even though she tried, and shut the door. Turning, I leaned back against it like a vampiric barricade.

Madison wasn't laughing, but her eyes glittered with humor.

I glared at her. "I'm going to do something terrible to you. Maybe I'll put snakes in your car when you're not looking."

Her mouth dropped open and her eyes widened. "Tell

me you're joking!"

"You won't know when or where they are or if you got them all!" I threatened. I wouldn't really do it.

"You suck." Her head and shoulders dropped in a sulk.

"Quite literally," I returned, glancing at the shut door over my shoulder and hoping that Madame Cliché was gone. Thinking that it was safe, I went back into my office and left Madison to think about snakes.

❰O❱

More than an hour later and Madison didn't look like she'd forgiven me for the snake thing as I left for the meeting at the Coven House. She barely even looked at me as I walked out the door, but I knew she would forgive me by the end of the night. She always did.

As I drove, my thoughts focused less on Madison and more on the meeting ahead of me and if I was truly going to be anything more than the extra person in the room. It just felt weird, like I was a conversational blankie.

I pulled into the Coven House's long driveway a few minutes early, but I saw that the police-issued SUV was already there. Many other cars lined the way, forcing me to park at the end. Last I knew, more than a dozen vampires called this place home and apparently everyone and their cars were in. I wondered how Johnston and Marlowe had managed to get such a good spot near the entrance. Did everyone rush home right after they'd gotten there?

As soon as I opened the car door, I caught a smell that I hadn't expected. It wasn't that it necessarily stood out as wrong, just surprising. But tonight wasn't the kind of night that I wanted a surprise. I was immediately on edge. For a moment, I tried to tell myself that smelling a hawk wasn't strange... except that birds were usually in the air, and creatures of any type tended to instinctively know they shouldn't set up camp near this place, even if the vamps didn't usually feast on local wildlife.

It turned out to be a good thing that I was edgy. If I hadn't been, I would have been caught terribly off guard by the shrieking ball of anger that flew at me out of nowhere. I was a lousy excuse for a preternatural being, but at least this time, it was a shifter and not a human that caught me unaware. That helped the wounded pride a little bit.

We crashed to the ground. The man made an avian shriek with his human mouth as his hands circled my throat. For an instant, I thought he must be an idiot. Why try to choke someone who doesn't breathe? Then I saw the strategy: he was holding me in place while pulling a stake from his pocket. He was a were-hawk and had the reflexes for it. That arm was up, ready to plunge the stake into my chest, in as much time as it took me to blink.

I threw my hands up and caught his arm before it reached me, but his other hand on my throat limited my reach. Fortunately, a vampire is consistently stronger than a shifter and once I got my hands on him, I could wrench him to one side and throw his aim away from getting close to my heart. His grip on my neck remained solid, however, and when I tossed him to the side, he took me with him.

So I threw my weight until I was on top of him. With one hand keeping his stake away from me, I used *my* other hand to pull *his* other hand away from my neck. I had the vague impression of a four-armed monster having convulsions, but it didn't linger too long. His knee hit me in the spine. At a different angle, it would have hurt more but it did enough to throw me forward. For that first instant, I nearly smothered him with my chest. (It was the most action I'd seen in a while, only ruined by the homicidal intent.)

Then the bastard bit me on the breast. I think I was more shocked than anything, and I tore myself away. We scrambled apart and glared at one another for a few moments. I was trying to figure out if I knew this guy and why he wanted to kill me. He just seemed to be analyzing the tactical situation.

He launched at me again. Now that I saw him coming, I sidestepped him easily. His fingers caught the edge of my shirt and dragged us both to the ground. This time, I recovered more quickly and punched him in the jaw. It put him flat on the ground while I got to my feet. I reeled back for a second strike but didn't land it before he leaned up and staked me in the thigh.

It felt like someone had lit me on fire. I screamed. Only one thing could make me feel that way, and I knew there was silver in the stake. He tore it free and blood oozed out. He pulled back, ready to stab again. Through the pain, I was ready to defend myself, but headlights pulled into the driveway. The shifter saw this and spooked, turning and sprinting away.

I wanted to go after him but a touch of silver had gotten into my system, and I could feel it, lingering in my thigh and trying to burn its way out. The car parked, and a young vampire hurried in my direction.

"Are you okay?" he asked with concern.

"Not particularly," I said. I gritted my teeth and the points of my fangs dug into my bottom gums. I couldn't seem to care. "Could you help me into the house?"

His face was full of questions, but we could easily sense one another's ages and some vampire manners never go out of style: you don't second-guess your elders without good reason. He didn't ask any of those questions and just helped me into the Coven House and into the sitting room where Jade was with the detectives.

All three of them were on their feet as they watched me limp in.

"What the hell happened?" Johnston was the first one

to ask.

"Nobody in the world likes me," I deadpanned as I dropped onto the sofa. After that, I gave them the quick-and-dirty version of events, which really was the only version there was.

"Right outside the door?"

"On coven territory?"

These two questions came simultaneously from Johnston and Jade. Neither of them sounded too happy and who could blame them? I detected a note of something else in his voice, however, but I couldn't place what it was. I knew Jade was upset not because of any particular expression but because she slipped into more antiquated language, like calling it territory rather than property. I let them vent while I just sat on the couch and bled in painful ways.

"My apologies," Jade said abruptly. "Can I get you anything? Do you want to see Abby?"

Abigail was an interesting character in the Coven House and one rarely seen, but she had a healer's touch and so was usually called when such things were needed. Vampires, though, didn't need it often.

I shook my head. I was at least pleased that one of them remembered me. "There wasn't much silver, so I doubt anything can be done except to wait it out." Besides, Abby creeped me out, so I wanted to avoid her.

Johnston—Vance—sat down beside me. Without asking, he examined the edges of the hole in my jeans. I stared at his hand, but he didn't seem to realize that I was surprised. His fingers gently pried apart the torn fabric and looked at the healing skin beneath it, while I was torn between looking at my leg and his hands.

The skin on my thigh was already clear and smooth again, but there were faint lines of silver where the wound had been, where it had settled in my veins. Meanwhile, his hand was warm. There was life in that hand. When his fingertips touched my skin, even briefly as it was, I could feel his pulse. It was like in that instant, the world around me vanished, and I couldn't hear anything but his heart beating and his lungs breathing. I heard it more loudly and more clearly than anyone else living.

"I don't know much about vampire healing," he said. His voice snapped me out of whatever little la-la-land I had wandered off to.

"I'll be fine," I said. My voice sounded a little hoarse.

"Perhaps we should reschedule this for another time," Jade suggested. I had to imagine she noticed the moment that had just passed, but she was too polite to say anything.

"That might not be a bad idea," Vance added.

I caught the look that Marlowe shot him, but *I* was polite enough not to take any undue notice of it. "No," I said. "We're all here. That would be silly. I'll be just fine."

Vance didn't look very content with the idea, but Marlowe didn't really give the appearance of caring either way. Then again, with a face like hers, it could be hard to tell what she thought. Jade, meanwhile, looked uncertain but didn't say anything more.

"I'll put this information into a report when we get back to the station and see if we can track down this hawk," he said. "But we are here, so perhaps we should finish our talk after all."

As the three of them delved into their interview, I made it my role in the matter to sink as deeply into this lovely couch as possible. If nothing else, you can credit vampires with having good taste. After all, when you live so long, why come out of it having learned nothing about what's comfortable and looks good? I appreciated Jade's taste because the former was never forsaken for the latter.

I kind of zoned in and out while they talked, given the

silver sparking that allergic, itchy feeling everywhere in my body.

I heard things here and there. Jade knew the second vampire from the picture, although she hadn't seen him in a while and didn't know where he was. I think there was also something else about attacking anyone over anything being 'so very unlike him.'

"Are you still with us?" Vance asked suddenly. It felt sudden. I felt his weight settle into the couch beside me once again, and the sound of his heart beating flooded my ears. I opened my eyes and rolled my head on the back of the sofa towards him.

"Barely," I murmured but smirked slightly. "See? I'm still alive."

He smiled. I still liked seeing it. "No, you're not," he teased, and I had to laugh.

"In my own way." Jade and Marlowe were still talking, so I had to wonder what he was doing over here with me. After a moment, his smile faded, and he looked away. I added my frown to things. "What is it?"

He shook his head and sighed. "I can't believe that you were attacked right in this damn driveway, and I didn't hear anything. Supernatural hearing, my ass," he said with a surprising amount of anger. Who was he mad at, I had to wonder.

I tried to offer what I thought would be a reassuring smile, but it wasn't like I was a camp counselor on my best days, let alone at moments like this. "It's all right," I said. "The driveway to this place is as long as the path into the Grand Canyon and even we have our limits, you know?"

"I guess so." I didn't think he sounded very convinced.

Before I could say anything more, Marlowe walked over. "We're done here," she said.

Vance looked up and nodded, getting to his feet. He

turned back to me. "You shouldn't drive yourself home," he said. His tone didn't seem like one that would take any argument and being naturally resistant, I wanted to argue.

"I'm fine," I said, toning down my knee-jerk reaction because he seemed earnestly concerned for my wellbeing. "I can drive."

"Maybe, but it seems like I wouldn't be doing much for my role in protecting and serving the community if I didn't insist that you let me drive you home."

Marlowe was frowning, or I thought she was. Again, with that face and all... I wondered if she didn't quite agree with his assessment. I wasn't sure if I agreed with it either, but I wasn't feeling up to arguing too much. "What about my car?"

Jade stepped in now. "At least let me do this much for you. I feel terrible that you were attacked on coven property. If you would be willing to trust us and leave your keys, I can assure you that we will get it back to your house in one piece."

I couldn't think of any reason to say no that wouldn't just be impossibly rude to the leader of the vampires in town, so I caved and nodded. We all made our polite farewells and went out to the car. I limped my way there but was well enough to do it without anyone's help, even though each step sent stinging pain up and down my leg. Silver was just evil. I tried to resist and ignore that thought as Vance drove us to my house and dropped me off.

Marlowe's presence was a small dark cloud of a warning that kept us from saying anything that wasn't business. Vance remained silent while she took my official statement as we drove. We finished right about the time we reached my driveway. I held off any personal farewells and went inside.

CHAPTER EIGHT

I got into the house and headed straight for the living room, where I promptly dropped myself face-first on the couch. This was one moment where that not needing to breathe thing actually came in handy. In truth, that was useful more often than you might imagine, depending on the extent of your imagination, I suppose.

My leg still hurt, but the pain had mostly faded. My system didn't work like any living body, but it seemed to have its own mystical way of working things out, and this was where most of the silver had gone by now.

After wallowing on the sofa for a bit, I flopped over and promptly fell on the floor because I misjudged the width of my own couch. Epitome of vampire grace that I was, I just stayed on my back on the floor, wedged between the sofa and the coffee table. Fishing in my pocket, I got my cell phone and called the office. After two rings, Madison picked up.

"Where are you?" she asked. It only took me a couple of moments to remember that the office had caller ID. Otherwise I would have to yell at her for not answering the phone in any sort of professional manner.

"Home," I replied, staring up at the popcorn ceiling. I still didn't know why they did that to ceilings. "This is where I'm going to be for the rest of the evening." I gave her a quick summary of the attack. I underplayed as much of it as I could so that she didn't worry, but she did it anyway.

She sighed. "Who did you piss off lately?" I could tell

that it was a rhetorical question, so I didn't bother to answer. Besides, I didn't really *have* an answer. "Do you want me to come home?"

I shook my head needlessly. "There's no need for that," I assured her. "I'm fine and just about healed already. One of us needs to stay at the office to hold down the fort, after all. I'll see you later." I hung up before she could argue with me. I loved her like she was my biological sister, but I just didn't feel like having her hover.

After hanging up, I laid on the floor for a while. Why did I do this? Even I wasn't sure, but it seemed like the thing to do and so there I was. I think I was just embarrassed that I had fallen off the couch, even if no one was there to see it.

Some time passed. I didn't really pay attention to how much. Vampires are better at that than most. The pain in my leg had pretty much gone away, leaving just a lingering ache. My phone rang. I was afraid it was Madison calling to check up on me after all of five minutes, though since I didn't know how long it had been, that was an unfair assessment.

I answered without looking at the ID, so I was really surprised when I heard Vance's voice on the other end. I sat up quickly and managed to not hit my head on the coffee table.

"Hey," I managed very eloquently.

"Hey," he echoed. At least I wasn't the only dumb one in this pair. "I was just calling to check in. Make sure you were doing okay and all."

At first, I tried to think of another way to say 'I'm fine' but when nothing came to me, I fell to the old standby. "I'm fine."

I thought that I could hear him nodding. "Good... Good..." he said and then one of those awkward silences dragged out between us. After a few moments of that, he finally filled the space when he said, "I know this is probably really presumptuous of me, but do you mind if I stop over?"

My brows rose on my face. "Sure?" I said, realizing as it came out of my mouth more like a question than a statement that it sounded kind of silly, so I repeated it with a little more emphasis. "Sure, that's fine."

"Good, I'll be there in about ten minutes."

I hung up and looked around my living room in a suspicious manner, like there was something in there that was going to explain what just happened. When I discovered there wasn't anything, I moved onto the moment of panic about making sure the place was in a state acceptable for company. Men were worse about the messy house thing, but Madison and I could destroy a place pretty well, too. Especially with the out all night and sleeping all day thing I had going on.

So, it was a mad dash to clean up the living room, tossing everything either into the trash or appropriate hiding places of rooms that I couldn't imagine he'd be going into. By the time I was done and making the final survey of my kingdom, there was the knock at the door.

The witty repartee started again right away.

"Hey," I said, standing back to wave Vance in. He smiled and stepped inside. I led the way back to the sofa. "Can I get you anything to drink?"

"Do you have anything that didn't come out of a vein?" he asked with a smirk.

I laughed. "Yes, I do. My roommate is a werewolf, and she doesn't do the liquid diet thing."

Vance nodded with a chuckle. "Water would be fine."

Getting up, I went into the kitchen. Once out of eyesight, I rolled my eyes at myself and wondered what I was doing. I wondered what he was doing. Maybe he really was just concerned about my welfare, though he had asked me out on a date. At least I think it was a date? Coffee was usually a date, wasn't it? Either way, I couldn't now escape that funny tingling feeling that he was more interested in me than I had thought after the coffee question, but then I knew that I didn't know him all that well so maybe I was reading him wrong.

I brought the water into the living room and gave it to him. We sat and stared at each other, or everything but, for a few minutes.

"How's the leg?" he finally asked.

"It's fine," I said automatically, looking down and realizing I hadn't even changed out of the bloody jeans. That had to be attractive. "Feels just like a bruise, minus all the pretty colors."

His eyes lingered on my thigh for a while longer, and I realized that I could hear his heartbeat again, and it was speeding up. Suddenly I missed having a pulse. I missed feeling the way the heart races over something exciting, over that instant when you realized the way someone was looking at you, or drawing near to someone, like the way he was suddenly leaning in towards me.

I couldn't seem to make myself move. I felt my mouth open as though I was going to say something, but no words came out. He moved slowly, giving me every opportunity to stop him, but I didn't. I just sat there and watched as he came towards me. If I breathed, it would have been caught dead center in my throat.

Then he kissed me, and all the somber nerves in my body electrified. The feeling was so intense that I almost felt as though I shared the feeling of life, what he had and I didn't, but we were sharing it in that moment. His kiss was very light, tentative. He was probably worried I was going to bite him for it, but hurting him was the last thing on my mind. Instead I wrapped my arms around his neck and pulled myself close. If it surprised him, it never showed.

His arms slid around my waist and pulled me even

closer. He was strong. My senses were filled with his scent. If I had been ambivalent about that before, now I found the power of it to be heady. It was masculine, the salty tang of sweat and that faint trace of cat. It was exotic and thrilling. The way he moved was dominant and powerful. I was swept under as his mouth opened and mine unconsciously did as well. The entire day, the entire week—hell, the entire room— melted from around me as he so easily and entirely claimed my mouth with his.

His body temperature rose and my body warmed with it, absorbing his heat. One of his hands slid into my hair, pinning me against the kiss, yet I didn't mind. In fact, I kind of liked it. Feelings I hadn't experienced in over a year were now stirring in me. I felt his hand slide from my hair to my neck. Skin against skin, it felt like he was on fire and nearly pulled me under.

I was on the verge of just saying 'to hell with it' and tearing off both our clothing when I was suddenly aware of a second heartbeat in the room. Dragging myself away, I turned to see Madison standing in the archway with her mouth hanging open.

"Oh shit," Vance murmured, pulling back and wiping his mouth. "I'll call you, Sadie." He made a hasty exit. I switched between looking at where he'd been and where Madison currently was. The front door shut.

"Sadie?" She laughed with surprise as she glanced back at the door and then came quickly to sit next to me, dropping her bag on the floor. "What was that?"

I stared at her. "And you were telling me that *I've* been single too long?" I took comfort in a little sarcasm. I could still feel his heat lingering in my body.

She pointed at me. "Don't change the subject!" she said. "Man, from the looks of things, it's a good thing I wasn't five minutes later. I would have seen a hell of a lot more of both of you than I ever wanted to." She grinned, wolfishly of course.

"Well, I might not have minded seeing more of him. He's quite good-looking."

"He is, isn't he?" I looked back towards the doorway, even though he was gone.

"I'm always glad when you take my advice, but you certainly move quickly," she commented. That grin wouldn't go away. Apparently, my making out with someone made her forgive the threat of snakes. Strange how that worked.

I held up my hands in defense. "It wasn't like I expected it. He called and asked if he could come by. I said yes before I even thought it through, and then he was here, and we were talking, and then he kissed me."

"And you didn't seem too eager to refuse," she teased.

"No, I wasn't." I wasn't going to lie, since that would have been pretty transparent. "It felt really nice."

Her grin turned into a warm smile. "I'm sorry I chased him off." She was sincere.

I smiled and shrugged, sinking into the back of the couch. "Cats and dogs," I said and if she'd taken a moment to inhale while gawking, she'd understand what I meant. "Probably for the best, though." I couldn't, however, put a lot of conviction into that statement. In fact, I found myself wishing that he'd come back, right up until the moment I passed out for the day.

Chapter Nine

I slid back into consciousness the next evening and right into a memory. It rose uncalled at the instant of waking. It was the closest thing to dreaming that I had done in years. It wasn't something I'd experienced often. It only seemed to happen when life was really intense.

My memory sent me flying back to the forties.

My sire, a vampire named Simone who saved me from starving to death during the Great Depression, and I were in Europe. We worked the night shifts helping nurse the soldiers injured in the second 'war to end all wars.' It was risky, being what we were, but unlike every stereotype ever, we still cared about people. Living beings. We didn't kill them or feed off anyone unwilling, and it was wartime. The entire nation was swept up in its fervor. We wanted to do our part.

We worked with the nuns in an orphanage during the Korean conflict.

Those are the places I went back to now in my dreams. Times of war. Of conflict. Of fighting and blood and anxiety.

The memories were short-lived but absolutely crystal clear. When consciousness fully wrestled me away from them, I was left with sorrow blanketing me. And fear.

The void filled abruptly with the electronic ringing of my cell phone. I tried to clear my mind as I rolled over and reached for it. I didn't recognize the number but answered it anyway. Maybe it was one of the hunters returning my voicemail, since I had yet to hear back from either of them. I was, however, very disappointed.

"Miss Stanton, this is Laurie Hendricks calling. I'm secretary for Frederick Hughes. He would like to invite you to a friendly debate with him about Cameron's Law on the Channel Thirty news tonight."

I hadn't been feeling awful enough from the memories so the universe decided to fuck with me and wake me up with this call. That was just a low blow.

"I'm not interested, thank you," I said with far more civility than I felt and even more than I thought I was capable of. That ended quickly when I hung up before she could get another word in. After a moment, the phone rang again with the same number, so I shoved it between the mattress and boxspring. I buried my head under my pillow until the ringing stopped.

Once it had, I rescued my phone and checked my messages. Neither of the hunters had called and there were just a couple standard messages from the office's daytime answering service. Then there was a message from Vance. If my heart still beat, it would've skipped a time or two.

"Hi, Sadie," he said. "I just wanted to apologize for running out like that last night. I just got really caught off guard. I swear I didn't plan for that, and I hope you're not angry at me. I'd really like to see you soon, perhaps at a time when your roommate isn't likely to walk in." He laughed. "Give me a call." He left his cell phone number and then hung up.

I wanted to call him right away but stifled the urge. I knew enough that it wouldn't be good to look too eager. Besides, I actually did have to get ready for work and then, you know, do some actual work.

So, I got myself cleaned up and dressed for the day. When I walked outside, I saw that Jade was as good as her word, although I was hardly surprised. My car sat in the driveway and my keys were in the mailbox. Risky, but then what was the option if no one was there to take them? It was good enough for me, and I just appreciated the effort, so I took the keys and got in.

The phone rang again as I drove to work. This time, I recognized the number as the Coven House so I answered without concern and technically broke the law in Connecticut by talking on a cell while driving, but what was life without a little danger? "Hello?"

"It's Jade," came the voice on the other end. As if I couldn't recognize that voice anywhere. "I simply wanted to see how you were doing, if you were feeling better after the attack last night. I am still so sorry that happened. I cannot believe the Coven House's wardens weren't closer to help you."

"Shit happens." I turned onto Currier Street. "I'm doing fine. All healed up and it was hardly the first person to ever try to kick my ass, so I'm not too traumatized. I appreciate the call, though." I paused. "I hope there hasn't been any more trouble?"

"Not that I've heard of, but the night is young."

That made me feel so much better.

☽O☾

There wasn't anything thrilling going on at the office. Madison had started before I got there, and there was little to report. There were no new hunter applications, which made me sad, but what could you do? I had thought I'd had an interview for the animator job I also had open, but Madison informed me that I was incorrect. Actually, she more informed me that I was getting addle-minded in my old age, but I let it pass.

With all of those matters seen to, I went into my office and did some boring paperwork. I was deep in the banal when my phone rang a few hours later.

How many bad things start with the ringing of a telephone?

It was Gabriel Raines, the alpha of the local pack. He didn't bother saying hello or anything like that. The first words he said were, "Have you heard?"

There was that moment of panic when I felt like there was something I should know but didn't. I had been buried in my office and hadn't heard much of anything since I'd come back here. I said as much to him. "No, what happened?"

He paused, and I could hear him breathe deeply. "It happened tonight. Practically just happened, the police are still on site and everything."

I felt my metaphorical blood go cold. "What happened?"

"One of my pack was out this evening with his kids, two of them, just seven and four years old. The little girl hasn't even had her first shift yet. Anyways, he was out with them, and it was the same story. A vampire came out of nowhere and attacked them. Well, he reacted like a father whose kids were in danger, Sadie." I could hear how upset he was, even as tightly controlled as he kept his tone.

"You don't have to go on the defense with me, Gabriel," I told him calmly. "Just tell me what happened."

Another deep breath. "He fought back, but this time, it was a brawl. The vampire didn't run off. My wolf killed him. Sadie, the vampire is dead, really dead. My wolf ripped his fucking head off when he lunged for the girl. I don't know what kind of shit this is going to cause now."

It had to have happened between the time Jade had called me and now, because I was certain that she would have mentioned this. "Your wolf had every right to protect his children," I said first, even as I felt my body go systemically numb. "I don't know what's going on. God, I wish I did, but I don't think there'll be any retribution from the coven. Jade knows something is wrong and that it's starting with the vampires. Everyone will understand the need to defend one's family."

"Does she really control every vampire in the coven?" he asked. I knew this wasn't something you could be comforted out of in just a few words, but it didn't sound like my reassurance had made any impact at all.

"No," I conceded, "but she does exert a lot of influence and vampires are not, by nature, entirely irrational."

He snorted. "No more than humans."

"*Or wolves.*"

"Point taken, but still, I think that I have a reason to be worried."

I nodded, whether he could see it or not. "I can't deny that," I said, "but I will do whatever I can to make sure that it doesn't become a problem." I heard him start to retort but cut him off before he got there. "A different kind of problem," I corrected. "I've been in pretty frequent contact with Jade lately, so I will talk to her again. We'll do what we can, I promise." I paused, making sure he had no immediate complaint on that. "You said the police have been called, right?"

"Right," he agreed.

"Okay, I've been talking to them a lot lately too, so I'll work it from that angle, as well," I promised. "It will be okay, somehow."

☾O☽

I had no idea if it was going to be okay. In fact, after hanging up, I spent about ten minutes staring at my desk and unraveling every scenario I could imagine, from everything just stopping and going away to an all-out turf war between the two biggest preternatural communities not just in Adelheid but the entire state, even country. Vampires accounted for nearly forty percent of the preternatural population in the US and wolves another thirty.

In reality, something in between was more likely, but I couldn't seem to rein in my anxious imagination. I couldn't figure out what it was I was going to do about it, either, but I was in debt, of a sort, to both the coven and the pack leaders to do whatever I could to avoid a war, so there I was.

My dream-memories jumped back to the forefront of my mind, and I suppressed a shiver.

I picked up the phone and called the Coven House. I was immediately transferred to Jade.

"You've heard," she said. I brushed off my sense of déjà vu.

"Yes, I don't suppose you have any better an idea of what's going on?"

I heard her swallow, and I knew that was a bad sign. You didn't hold onto many reflexive habits when you got to be her age unless you were upset. She would never show it outwardly in any other way, but that was enough of a sign to get me even more worried because, really, it wasn't like I wasn't freaking out enough.

"No," she said. This was a useful conversation so far. "I know as much as you know, I'm sure, which is sadly limited. I do not blame the wolf for what he did, but not everyone here shares my opinion."

"Are you having trouble with the other vampires?" It was a question I needed the answer to but hadn't wanted to ask.

"Not yet," she replied honestly. I knew it was an honest answer because few in a position of power like hers would admit something like that. They would lie and say that everything was fine and under control. "However, there is dissatisfaction growing in the house. A lot of it stems from fear. We don't know what's happening, or if it could happen to any of us."

I, however, was not old enough to have outgrown reflex, so I inhaled thoughtfully without actually thinking about it. "Do you have any idea of what it might be? I mean, what's going on with the attackers?"

There was a long pause. "I have nothing of substance," she finally said. "The only thing that comes to mind is from lore, legends, and myths, the old wives' tales of the vampire kind, you know?"

Every species had them, and their reliability tended to be the same. Still, when you had nowhere else to start, it was as good a place as any. "What do the tales say?"

"I'll need to speak with our historian, but from what I remember, there have been occasions when vampires have just gone crazy. It's usually a blood fever, but it means they try to feed and gorge themselves."

"Which hasn't been happening," I felt the need to state what we both already knew.

"Right," she agreed. "I can't think of anything without that. We're vampires, so it's always about blood. You know that as well as I do. I cannot imagine what would possess any vampire to attack without trying to *feed*."

That made more than two of us, I was sure. "Tell me more about what's going on in the Coven House, and what you think might happen."

There was another long pause. "It's hard to explain, because right now, it is just a feeling rather than anyone taking action. Few people are saying anything to me, which is also strange. You haven't spent much time here, but it is a surprisingly noisy place." Her laugh was quiet, but still cultured even in her concern. "I know that would probably shock a lot of people, but it's true. It's grown quiet over these past few days, however. Less of them are speaking to me, or to each other. I get the sense they are beginning to distrust one another. We aren't pack, Sadie. Vampires do not have that inherent trust and loyalty the shifters seem to. It takes work for us, and everyone seems to be looking at everyone else like they are going to go crazy at any moment and murder everyone else in the house."

She sighed in another show of agitation. "It is worst across the ages. The young ones are looking sidelong at the elders, because they distrust the power that comes with our age, or that the elders can be awake when the younger ones cannot be. The youth fear that we will wake before they do and kill them in their sleep."

"That's just what this city needs," I mumbled, "an outbreak of patricide."

"No one wants that," Jade agreed. Her voice had grown even softer and sounded almost apologetic. "They even seem to lose faith in our wardens, thinking they can't protect us. I will admit that the attack on you didn't help that. Now, we worry about the pack making any preemptive strikes."

I was counting on Gabriel to have better control over his wolves than Jade had over her vampires, although I wasn't blaming her for that. I understood how it worked. "I don't think that will happen," I said. "At least not yet. Gabriel sounds more worried that the vampires are going to do something in revenge for the death today."

"I don't think we're coming to that yet, either," she said. "Quite frankly, I think I'm more worried about us attacking each other." She paused again. "May I ask a favor?"

I had a sudden uprising of a new kind of dread. "Ask," I said, "and if it's something I am able to do, then I will do it."

For long moment, I waited for her question. "As I said, they do not seem to trust the wardens as much as they once did, but we need to be secure in ourselves. We need to know that the Coven House is at least as safe as it might be. I suppose this isn't as much a favor as a job, because I would like to hire you to check the perimeter of the house and grounds."

She paused again. "I guess the favor would be asking you to return after what already happened, but perhaps prepared this time. I simply think having someone as respected as you, and yet not a member of pack or coven, unaffiliated, could go a long way to easing their minds."

That wasn't what I had been expecting. I couldn't say the idea thrilled me, but if I was going in with shields up, I'd be better off than last time. And I wasn't sure I was in a position to turn down work, as well as a chance to assist my community.

"Sure," I said. "I will come by later tonight and see what I can do."

"Thank you." She sounded relieved. "I will see you later tonight then."

Chapter Ten

"You know, I'd been thinking of doing something to help me relax tonight," I lamented from where I laid very unprofessionally on the couch in the waiting room. Madison was behind her desk, working away while I sulked. The sound of her fingers hitting her keyboard echoed over my self-pity. "I was gonna go to the gym pool and swim for a while."

"You still could," she commented. I couldn't tell if she was impatient with me or feeling as stressed by events as I was.

It suddenly occurred to me that there had been three attacks. Against werewolves. She was a werewolf.

I pushed myself up on my elbows and looked at her. Her blue eyes were very intense on her screen, lips pursed slightly. The girl looked more like a Midwestern cheerleader than a werewolf secretary.

"Are you worried?" I asked quietly.

"Yes." She didn't look away from the screen. I saw her type something, frown, hit one key many times—backspace— and then type again.

When it repeated, I got off the couch and walked up behind her.

"This will get figured out," I said as reassuringly as I could, wrapping her in a hug from behind and leaning my head against hers. "I don't know how yet, but we will. We'll keep you safe, Madison."

She sniffled and put her hands over mine.

☾O☽

An hour later, I headed out for my 'security guard' job.

Arriving at the Coven House, I parked in the same place as last time, but this time, I checked for psychopaths as I got out. I smelled nothing on the wind and didn't hear the beating of any hearts. Nobody here but us dead folk.

I felt out of my league as I began walking the boundaries of the coven's property. I knew enough of the house and the town to know where the border was. I planned to check the grounds first and then check closer to the building. To be honest, I wasn't entirely sure exactly what I was looking for, but I figured if something seemed out of place or suspicious, I would at least recognize it.

I hoped. Jade hoped.

Hope was a lousy plan, or so I'd heard it said.

Everything seemed as it should be. I could smell hints of small animals and even, as I got closer, hear their little beating hearts. Not many, but some. There was also that very faint lingering scent of the grave that permeated wherever a vampire spent a lot of time. It was too pale for anyone but shapeshifters and vampires to pick up, and even most shifters wouldn't know what it was unless they were familiar with it.

Finishing a full circuit of the outer edge, I was just beginning to move inward when I heard a heart—a louder, larger heart—and smelled something new.

It was a strange scent. I couldn't recall ever smelling anything like it before, and I froze, listening to the breeze shifting in the trees. It wasn't human. It was something more. It was moving quickly. In fact, it was moving very quickly, with almost vampire speed. I realized it was coming up behind me, and I spun to face it, but found myself level with the muzzle of a gun and a very tall, very angry-looking woman staring down its length.

"What are you doing here?" she demanded.

"What are *you* doing here?" I demanded back.

Her eyes narrowed, and I watched her tongue run over her teeth. She wasn't a vampire but apparently shared a habit or two. "You look familiar." That part caught me off guard, because it really wasn't what I guessed would come next in this situation. She lowered her gun a little and peered more intently at my face. "You were on the news."

I hated to think of the opinion a person might gather from seeing me going head-to-head with Hughes. "From time to time," I replied cautiously, still wondering who this woman was.

She shook her head. "A lot," she corrected, "a year ago."

"Yes, I was." It was on archive footage all over the place, so it wasn't like there was any use in trying to deny it, even if I wanted to. "So, you know who I am, but I still don't know who the hell you are or why you're running vampire ground with a heartbeat. Some people might call that dangerous."

"Some might," she agreed with a small, dark smile. She put the gun back into a shoulder holster, and I was relieved. A bullet in my brain could kill even me. At least I could say being on television had been good for one thing now. "My name is Dakota. I'm a hunter by trade, but I take the jobs I can get. A corpse in the house hired me to check things over, given the present climate. Figured if there was something shitty going on out here, I could take care of it."

I wondered if I'd seen her resume cross my desk, but I didn't think so. My gut said she wasn't the 'apply for a job' kind. "I am going to assume that it wasn't the coven leader, because that's what she asked *me* to do."

Dakota shook her head. "Wasn't her," she agreed,

although she didn't supply who her employer had been either. "I didn't think you did this kind of work." Her every word had an edge that bothered me, yet without being able to point to any one thing specifically.

"I take what jobs I can get." I threw her words back to her.

She seemed able to appreciate that and revisited that mildly frightening smile. "I guess the rumors about in-fighting are true then."

I tilted my head. "Inside the Coven House?" I asked, feeling the need to clarify.

Dakota nodded.

"It's possible," I conceded, "but I don't like to discuss that business with folk I don't know, especially ones that have already pulled a gun on me once tonight."

"I was told to treat anything strange with caution." She was nonplussed. "You seemed strange enough to warrant it."

"I've been called worse." I chuckled, although inwardly, I was more concerned than ever.

Jade hiring me while some other vampire down the ranks hired Dakota was not a good sign, presuming her story was true. I didn't yet have evidence it wasn't. In fact, it seemed to confirm Jade's concerns. The last thing the vampires in this town needed was to break apart in their own ranks as unfavorable public opinion and the pack were possibly turning against them.

After a moment, I realized she was staring at me.

"What?" I asked suspiciously.

"You still working for the betterment of all preternatural kind?" She had a very abrupt way of changing the subject.

I nodded slowly. "I suppose you could say that. I like to do my part and help out the community, which is why I'm here tonight."

A strange expression flashed through her eyes. It was like she was weighing my words, evaluating me. "You had a good reputation a year ago," she said. "A lot of the preternaturals trusted you, so I suppose you can still be trusted to not be lying to me. I'll tell you this much. I wasn't just hired for this, but also to try to track down some of the missing vampires. You know, the ones who did the earlier attacks." She paused. "The ones with their heads still attached."

That brought both of my brows up. "Someone doesn't have faith in the police, either?"

Dakota smirked with a 'are you serious?' kind of look. "No," she said bluntly. "Not many of us do. You should know that."

Right then, I figured out what it was about her that annoyed me. She was talking to me like I was a kid. She was no vampire, so I was probably older than she was, but it seemed like every other statement out of her mouth treated me like a five-year-old. That was obnoxious, considering I hadn't been five in…ninety years? Who keeps track at this point.

"Yes," I said dryly, "I do know that. Still, neither side is ever going to have any trust, faith, or respect in one another if we don't give each other a chance. The cops are working on it, and I'm working with them. They aren't just sitting on their hands, hoping we kill each other off."

"If you say so," she replied. That was apparently as much ground as she was going to give me. "I'll try to stay out of their way, but I've still got a job to do." She started to turn away but paused, looking back. "Try not to cross my gun sights again, okay?" She smirked and turned, leaping into a run. For a brief moment, I thought it looked like she turned into a large cat, but she was gone so fast I wasn't sure what I had seen. No shifter changed form that easily, did they? Certainly none I ever knew.

Either way, she was gone now, and I had a job to finish, too. Which I did, but nothing else happened that proved nearly as interesting as my encounter with the strange woman, Dakota.

CHAPTER ELEVEN

Without a doubt, being present at an autopsy is one of the most unpleasant things to experience. I've been told it's bad enough with the average human olfactory sense, but try being in there when you've got a sense of smell way above average. It's just miserable, but there's valuable information to be learned in the procedure, and Vance had been kind enough to get me in, so I was sucking it up (literally and metaphorically) and attending.

When he had called me shortly after I got back from the Coven House to invite me to the autopsy of the dead vampire, I thought a date at the morgue sounded kind of strange, but I was willing to go with it.

Adelheid had its own satellite location to the OCME, or Office of the Chief Medical Examiner. There was an ME who worked full-time there and handled all preternatural cases for the area, as he was specialized in supernatural medicine. His name was Carl Wright, and he was in his forties. He knew all kinds of things, both medically related and otherwise, but had a reputation for being remarkably humorless. In truth, I didn't think it was so much a lack of humor but being too literal. It just took a special brand of joke for him to get it, and he rarely found me as funny as I found myself.

"So far, everything looks normal," Wright was saying.

No one would ever guess he was calling a vampire's innards normal. He had already performed the surface examination and had now made the Y incision, hauling out organs like most people sling around ground beef. Even I felt a little queasy at the sight, and that wasn't even counting the fact that the head was on a separate table. "I don't imagine anything surprising will be found here, though."

"What do you mean?" Vance asked. I gave him credit for being a lot less green around the edges than I imagined I must have looked, and he had no choice but to keep breathing.

Wright dropped what I guessed was a liver on the scale and replied without looking at either of us. "Vampires aren't alive, so whatever is going wrong isn't likely to be something in their bloodstream or body. There is no circulation to pump it through. If there's anything to be found in an autopsy, it will be in the brain."

I had my hand loosely over my mouth, trying not to look at the bloody bits. It looked like the red cells had coagulated and just stayed where they were, forever. God, was that really what was inside me? "Why bother with all this at all, then?" I asked, feebly hoping that maybe he'd stop because my question was clearly brilliant.

"One must be thorough," he replied blandly. "There is always that chance I'm wrong, and even if I'm right, if I don't do everything, someone will be asking me why I didn't." He paused. "And...I could be wrong. There is some element of what science can't define that takes place in vampires. Something could be in the blood and gotten to the brain somehow."

"Right," I mumbled.

"Would that be magic?" Vance murmured with amusement.

"Magic is just science that hasn't been explained," the magical vampire replied.

Wright didn't reply to our comments. Then again, he was human. He might not have heard us.

"Do we all smell that bad on the inside?" I couldn't stop

myself from asking.

"What?" Wright asked, finally meeting my eyes with a confused look. It got through to him a moment later. "Oh, I don't even notice anymore."

I had trouble imagining ever being used to such a smell, but maybe that was just me. I didn't bother repeating the question. Wright kept on with his work, I kept on feeling miserable, and Vance kept on being amused at my misery. All in all, it wasn't a very productive evening for me until after Wright moved to the other table and started up the bone saw, pulling off the skullcap, which was another experience I could have passed on. The noise had gone straight through me and made my joints ache.

Wright pulled the brain out. I tried to not look at the head while he worked, but it was hard to turn away. The face was... It was hard to describe what a face looks like when it's attached to a head that's not attached to anything else. There was also something almost familiar about the face, although I couldn't place it. I didn't want to keep looking till I remembered either, especially since maybe I didn't really recognize anything.

"Well, now, this is interesting," Wright commented as he set the brain down for an examination. His brows furrowed. It was the first sign of surprise or curiosity I had seen since coming here.

"What is it?" Vance asked after a moment, when it was obvious no more commentary was forthcoming.

"I'm not entirely sure." Wright shook his head. He took samples for further tests, and the gross factor exceeded new heights. "It just doesn't look right."

Feeling useful, I commented, "It's the brain of a long-time corpse. How right could it possibly look?"

Vance smirked. I appreciated that *he* thought I was funny. It sailed right past Wright, naturally.

"There is a particular way that the vampire brain looks. Unlike most things with your kind, this doesn't change with age. No one knows why. This brain, however, doesn't look right, but we won't know more until we can take a better look and run some tests."

"Do you think we are looking at some kind of illness, then?" Vance ventured.

"I can't say at this point," Wright replied. "I don't know what it is I'm looking at in the first place. It could simply be an abnormality with *this* vampire's brain. We'll run some tests on the brain tissue, as well as the blood. I'll let you know when I know more."

Vance and I hung around while he finished up a few more things, but nothing else of interest happened and we left. Wright was probably glad to see us go, if he even noticed.

"You seemed kind of freaked out back there," Vance commented once we were in the car, fastening seatbelts. He'd given me a ride there so was now kind enough to give me a ride back.

"No one really wants to see that close into how they work," I replied. "I guess that proves even truer when your workings are particularly gross, like when you're the walking dead."

He smiled. "I think you look pretty good for a corpse," he complimented.

I couldn't help but laugh, even though there wasn't much mirth to it. "I look exactly the same as the day I died," I said ruefully. "I haven't even cut my hair, although part of that is because, if I do, I'm stuck with it."

Silence drew out for a while, and I wondered if I had lost him somewhere. He finally broke it, though, and asked, "How did you become...what you are?"

"A vampire?" I supplied for him.

He nodded.

This was sort of a vampire litmus test. If someone wanted to date you, you told them how old you really were. If they still wanted to date you, it was off to a good start.

"I was born in nineteen-eighteen." I paused and looked sidelong at him. He shot me a quick look with brows raised but didn't say anything, so I kept going. "My father died in World War I, so my mother and I moved in with my grandparents. They died a few years later, and my mother died when I was sixteen. By this time, the country was deep into the Depression. There were debts, and the house was lost.

"I basically lived on the streets and struggled for three years. I then met a woman named Simone Belmont." I smiled a little with nostalgia, looking out the window. "She liked me, for whatever reason. I asked why, but she never told me. She gave me a choice: be a vampire or not. The 'not' part really equated to starving to death, so I agreed." I turned my gaze back to him.

He looked very focused as he drove, like he was taking it all in. "What happened to Simone?"

Now, I smiled. He was taking it well. That was a good sign. "She and I went our separate ways in the sixties. I wanted to explore. We kept in touch for a while, but time and all that. I traveled a lot."

"You've not seen her since?" he asked, sounding genuinely curious and almost...concerned that I hadn't seen my sire again. It made some small, warm thing open up in the center of my chest.

"We got together again for a little while in the nineties. I was going by the name Marie Daniels at that time. Simone..." I shook my head and sighed. "She wasn't the same. Something had changed her, but she wouldn't admit it or tell me what. She was bitter, and it was hard to be around her, so we split up again. I haven't heard from her since."

We drove in silence for a couple minutes before he

finally said, "You're almost a *hundred* years old?"

I laughed, forgetting for a few moments what was going on around us. "Yes."

"Does that make you a cougar?" He flashed me a crooked smile.

I laughed again.

Chapter Twelve

After our hopping date at the morgue, both of us had to get back to work.

I walked back into the office and Madison spared me a glance before turning back to her computer, but I saw her smirking. "Have a fun time at the autopsy? Did you have some undead-dead communing going on?"

"You're a laugh riot," I said dryly. "All I know is that it smells very bad."

"I would imagine so. You said Detective Johnston is a shifter, right? It couldn't have been much fun for him either."

"He is, and I doubt it, but he's also had more opportunities to get used to it," I said. "So, anything happen, or happening, here that I need to know about?"

Now she tore herself away from the screen. "Not as of yet," she said. "Thankfully, it's been quiet here. I'm perfectly happy with quiet. Too much going on lately as it is." She shook her head with an uncharacteristic sigh before turning back to work. "I would be happy if it went back to you being the only dead body I hear much about."

I outright rolled my eyes and grabbed my mail off her desk, shuffling through envelopes as I walked into my office and shut the door behind me.

I was almost to my desk when I realized...

...I wasn't alone.

Blinking, I looked up and saw Dakota—that weird

woman from earlier—sitting in the chair in front of my desk. I saw her, we held gazes for a moment, and then my brain caught up with itself and I jumped.

"What?" I gasped, looking between her and the door. Madison hadn't told me there was someone waiting. She never sent people into my office to wait. They stayed out front until I was there. She hadn't given any hint or acted like she knew. So... "How? Where? What?"

"Eloquent as always, I see," Dakota drawled with a small, amused smirk. The amusement was clearly at my expense.

I looked at the window at the back of my office. It was closed and latched. The plants on the sill were undisturbed.

"How the hell did you get in here?!" I finally exclaimed, tossing my mail on my desk.

"Maybe I'll tell you someday." The smirk wouldn't go away. "For now, I just came to talk."

I grunted and walked around to sit behind my desk. You could startle a century-old vampire, but it was hard to scare us. I wasn't gonna sweat her. I didn't really think she was out to do me harm, and I wanted to know why she was here...and how. I stared at her over my desk, and she just stared back. If this was a verbal game of chicken, I had a good feeling I was gonna have to be the one to break.

"Talk about what?"

"What's going on in this town," she stated plainly. "It's building hard and fast into one of those things that will fuck us all royally if we don't get on top of it. I like to work alone, but there's areas that aren't my forte. They may be yours."

I listened, nodding slowly. What she said made sense, but my not-beating heart was still shivering from the shock she'd given me. "You're probably right about that. Tell me what you can and I'll tell you what I can." I paused, a slight feeling rising in my chest that urged a sort of alpha match and establishing dominance. I couldn't really explain it, but I felt the need to assert my authority. Okay, I could explain it. "Since you're the one who did the breaking and entering, you start."

I saw her lips twitch. "Alright," she said. "I can agree to that." She cracked her knuckles, and the sound echoed in my office, making me wince. "I was hired by one of the younger vampires in the Coven House. They are terrified of the older ones right now."

"Jade mentioned that," I said. "They are afraid the old ones will wake up first or go to sleep later and take them out."

"Right. So, some of the kids are taking matters into their own hands. The one that could afford me hired me to check around the house. I don't really know what they thought I would find, but I agreed to look. Just in case."

It occurred to me that she very carefully didn't use pronouns, so I couldn't guess male or female for who hired her.

"I didn't find anything," I said. "Did you?"

"Just you."

"Right."

"Anyway. So. That's that. I also know that the latter two vampires involved in the attacks were coven, although not long-time. The first one wasn't."

Again, this matched up with what I knew. What little I knew.

"The coven's wardens are taking turns going out and looking for the two vamps that didn't get their heads ripped off," she went on. "They haven't found them."

I snorted and rubbed my neck. "Vampires are pretty hard to find when we don't want to be found."

"You don't have to tell me."

We were both quiet for a moment before something occurred to me. "Hey, in your dealings with the coven and vampires and such, have you heard mention of a guy named Walter Warren?"

Her brows knit as she shook her head. "Can't say that I have. Why?"

"His sister has reported him missing, but she also called me because she thought he might have been turned. Guess he's been talking about vampires a lot lately."

"Maybe he was turned by a non-coven vampire," Dakota pointed out.

I knew that was possible, certainly. "Well, while you're working with the coven, keep an ear out, perhaps?"

She tilted her head slightly, perhaps considering whether or not she wanted to do me a favor that wasn't related to our present community difficulties, but then nodded once. "Sure."

"Are you in much contact with the pack?" she asked.

"Here and there," I replied. "As far as I know, they aren't experiencing the same dissension. But then again, they are being attacked and not the attackers. That tends to make people get closer." I paused. "You haven't been hired by any one of them, then?"

"Not about this," she said. "Raines did want me to find his wife, just to make sure she was alive and okay."

I raised my brows. I didn't realize he'd gone as far as that, although the community was pretty aware of the fact his wife had just run off without leaving a word. Packed it up and was gone. It had torn him apart.

"Did you?"

"I did," she said. "I let him know she was okay."

I could only imagine that it was difficult for him to not find out where she was, but something in the way Dakota talked about it said she would not give away the woman's location. After all, leaving a spouse the way she did was rude but not criminal.

She got to her feet. "Well, this has been great, but I gotta get back out there."

"Dakota," I said, causing her to turn back to me. "My office is looking for a hunter. Not to work as an employee but a contractor. You'd have an office, and Madison to handle paperwork, but still be your own boss and all."

She arched her brow. "I'll think about it." Turning back to the door, she opened it and walked out. An instant later, I heard Madison shriek with surprise. Dakota turned her head over her shoulder and winked at me before walking out. I heard the front door open and shut.

"Sadie!"

☾O☽

Nothing for the rest of my evening was nearly as interesting as it had all started. I had another interview to conduct for the animator spot, which had a passable candidate but not one I was thrilled with.

I had Madison chastising me for not kicking Dakota out or calling the police on her, but I just ushered her away. After all that, we finished out the night's work in a far more boring way before I headed home and got to sleep.

Little did I know then what was going to be waiting for me the next day.

Chapter Thirteen

The day began like any other.

I woke up, and I was grateful for that. Technically, I lived again. I've been told that when in the 'daylight coma,' we vampires are basically corpses that don't decompose. Fortunately, I've never been awake-alive to see it on another. It really wasn't something I was eager to do, either, because no one wants to see too much about their own workings. (I think I might have covered this during the autopsy.)

Anyway. The day began. I didn't hear about any more attacks, so I proceeded with my day as usual. I eventually ended up at the office.

That's when the day went sideways.

I found both Vance and Marlowe sitting in my front office. Neither of them looked happy to see me. Well, really, neither of them looked happy at all. Madison looked nervous. That was a really bad sign.

"What's going on? Has another vamp attack happened?" I asked, my eyes jumping between them all like a three-player tennis match.

"May we speak in your office?" Marlowe asked, getting to her feet. Vance did so a moment after her, but he looked… embarrassed?

"Of course." I swallowed hard and led them into my office, exchanging a glance with Madison as I passed her. I tried to smile, but I was sure it came off as pained.

Once we were in the next room and the door was shut, I turned to face them expectantly. I didn't bother to sit, and neither did they. I just stared at them until one of them spoke, which was Marlowe again.

She handed me a picture. I knew in a moment that the person in the picture was dead. You just had a sense for these things as a vampire. I frowned as I studied it. There was something familiar about the blonde woman, although it was taking me a moment to—

"That bitch!" I exclaimed, before I realized what I'd said while looking at what I'd seen. I turned my attention back to the cops. "She's dead?"

"Do you recognize the woman in the photo?" Marlowe asked blandly.

I knew cops had to be double sure of things, but it did sound like a stupid question. I didn't say that aloud, of course. "Yes. I'm pretty sure this is the woman who attacked me. I mean, I didn't see her for long, so I guess I can't be totally sure...but I'm pretty sure." I handed the picture back to her.

Vance finally spoke up then. "She was found dead this afternoon along the side of I-three-ninety-five," he said darkly.

"Was she in a car accident?" I asked, confused. If she was found on the side of the highway, that seemed likely?

"No," Vance said, although he didn't elaborate.

"She was murdered," Marlowe said. "So far, the evidence is suggesting a vampire did it."

I opened my mouth to ask if they thought this was connected to the other attacks, but Marlowe answered what I had yet to ask.

"Not frenzied," she said. "We don't see a connection."

I deflated, although it having been a part of the series would have been worse news...maybe. I wasn't sure. This news was bad enough as it was. Actually, as I thought about it a moment longer, I wasn't sure if it could get worse.

This was bad.

Marlowe cleared her throat, and I snapped back to the moment.

"We found a note in her pocket," Marlowe went on, pulling an evidence bag out of her jacket pocket and handing it to me.

It had a time, date, and place.

It was my appointment time with the Whites.

"What…" I began, even more confused. "What does this mean?" I didn't even look up at them this time, just stared at the piece of paper with the handwritten note. There was something almost mesmerizing about that handwriting, too. It wasn't just the content but the aesthetic, as well. It was almost…familiar.

"I think that's pretty obvious," Marlowe said dryly. "She was sent."

"Sent," I repeated. What was it about the writing… Blinking, I looked up and met her eyes. "Sent?" More blinking. "So, someone hired her to come after me specifically? It wasn't just some racist spur-of-the-moment bullshit?"

Marlowe shook her head. "It doesn't seem like it," she said. "It looks like it was planned."

"Who would send a fucking human against a vampire?" I said, dumbfounded.

"We need to go over your statement from after the attack with you and find out where you were just before dawn last night," Vance said. I knew this had to be hard for him, but I wasn't feeling overly sympathetic.

I stammered for a moment. "Am… Am I a suspect?"

"Of course you are," Marlowe replied. Her condescension was getting old. "It appears this woman attacked you and was later killed by a vampire. You're a vampire with good reason for a grudge. We can't ignore that."

"Right... Right," I said, frowning at her. "I was, uh..." I thought back to the night before. "I was here pretty late, and then I went home and to bed."

"Can anyone verify that?"

"Madison should be able to verify most of it," I said. "She was here with me until I left, and got home soon after me..."

Marlowe nodded. "We'll talk to her."

They only stayed for a few minutes more while we discussed my attack and the statement I had made. I think they did most of the talking. I was just numb. But they couldn't have any evidence against me since I didn't do it. Their reasoning made sense, so I tried to not take it personal. But, you know, being accused of murder is sort of personal.

Once they left, I sat down hard behind my desk and just stared at the floor.

I wasn't sure how much longer it was before Madison came in, but I was sure it was a little while since they had wanted to talk to her, too. When she did come in, she looked worried as well and hurried over to me. "Sadie?" she said, almost like she was worried I was about to go psycho or something.

"This wasn't how I expected my day to start," I said with a weak smile lacking any actual humor.

"They can't have any evidence, so they're just here to rule you out," she said, sounding more confident in that than I did. But, of course, she was right. They had to do their due diligence, which meant talking to me about these things.

It still didn't really make me feel any better.

Chapter Fourteen

I t got worse.

I would have thought that being called a murder suspect would be the main low point of the night, but that wasn't the case. Some hour or two later, though I wasn't keeping track, we had visitors to the office. Unexpected, unwanted visitors.

It had been the shouting that lured me swiftly from my office, and when I saw the cause, I almost slammed the door shut again.

Standing in the middle of my front office was Frederick Hughes. He had a camera crew behind him, and there was a shouting match taking place between he and Madison. There was a woman sitting in one of the waiting room chairs, looking suspended on the line between uncomfortable and angry. Caught between fight and flight.

"What's going on out here?" I demanded. My tone was even, but I spoke loud enough to make sure I was heard. I couldn't let them see me rattled, certainly not this blowhard.

Hughes turned to me with a sanctimonious smile that I wanted to claw right off his face. "Ah, Miss Stanton," he said, immediately bringing his volume back down and turning away from Madison like she'd never been there at all. "What a pleasure it is to meet again."

I didn't rise to it. "I'm sure. What can I do for you, Mister Hughes?" Suddenly, I felt like I did over a year ago, when the lights and cameras were turned on me, and I was the voice of more than one species, where everything I said and did reflected on an entire community of people. I could feel Madison practically vibrating to my left, but at least she was quiet. It wasn't that I didn't understand, but emotional reactions weren't going to help.

I'd learned that lesson, and hard, a year ago.

"I figured that I couldn't have a balanced account of matters without talking to the...opposing side," he drawled. "What do you think, Miss Stanton? What's making you people go crazy?"

Sensing a threat, my fangs tried to descend while my mouth was still closed, but I was able to bring them back up. "I do not know what has happened to the *individuals* that have committed these recent assaults," I said in my most reporter-ready voice. It was almost frightening how easily it came back. I didn't need to blink, so I didn't. It tended to unnerve people subtly, eventually, and I needed every advantage I could get. Or try to get.

He steamrolled right along. "But you can't deny that something has gone wrong with the vampires."

"I can't deny something has affected these particular vampires," I said. I wasn't going to let him bait me, damn it. The verbal sparring part I was a little rusty on, so I had to focus and make sure I didn't reply too quickly to anything. Every response had to be measured over each word. "But I do not believe you can judge the entire species on the actions of a small number, any more than I can say all humans have 'gone wrong' simply because some of them shot at each other in New York City this year."

"You can hardly compare humans with...your kind." He made sure to cram as much insult into that hesitation as possible.

From the unknown woman, I heard a low, "You son of a..." I silenced her with a look, but Hughes had already turned.

"Well, you sound like a woman with an opinion,"

Hughes declared happily. He eyed her up and down. She was dressed in dress slacks and a white button-down, hair short but styled, and she glowered at Hughes. "You look...awfully *normal* to be here."

I jumped back in and tried to regain control of the conversation, feeling a sudden desperation to keep him from targeting anyone else. I didn't know this woman and didn't need a brawl in my waiting room show up on the damned six o'clock news. "Mister Hughes, I think I'm the one you came here to see—"

It was too late. He had already smelled blood in the water.

"And what sort of creature are you?" Hughes asked her.

"None of your business," she drawled.

Hughes grinned. "What, are you too ashamed to tell me?"

Madison sat down hard and looked at the top of her desk, which I was grateful for. It left me with only one loose cannon in the room.

"I'm not ashamed of anything," the other woman said. Suddenly, she smiled sweetly. Too sweetly. "I talk to the dead," she said, leaning forward and holding his gaze. "And frankly, I think much better of their rotting corpses than I do about you, Mister Hughes."

She leaned back again, folded her arms, and pointedly looked away.

Hughes made a 'hrmph' sort of sound and turned away. "I guess you never can tell," he muttered.

I sighed slightly with relief, but that still left the biggest problem standing in the middle of the room.

"I would kindly ask you to leave, Mister Hughes," I said tightly. "This is a place of business, and you're disrupting our work." It wasn't ideal to kick the press out of anywhere, but I didn't have any choice. I couldn't let this go on. He wasn't here for any real reason. He just wanted to wind us up and see what happened.

"Are you trying to hide something, Miss Stanton?" Hughes asked.

"Not at all," I replied easily, "but you are disrupting my flow of business, and I have the right to ask you to leave to let us go about our work." I gestured towards the door, moving to put myself between Hughes and the other women.

He looked like he was going to argue but seemed to think better of it. I would have hoped it was a moment of humanity where he realized he was just poking wounds with sticks but, realistically, he probably thought it would look bad on camera to push me.

"Of course," he said smoothly. Then was gone, but he left an emotional wake like a tornado had ripped through everyone's spirits.

"I'm sorry, Miss Stanton," the woman said. "I should have kept my mouth shut."

I took one of those breaths. It helped calm me on the inside, getting me closer to feeling as easy as I looked. "It's all right," I replied. "You can't let a bastard like that get under your skin, though. It's not going to do anyone any good."

She nodded. "I know, but it's very difficult."

"Believe me," I said, "I know."

I walked around to Madison. I knelt down to look up into her face, finding her gnawing on her bottom lip.

"You're going to put a hole in it if you keep doing that," I told her quietly, and then nodded for her to come into my office with me, which she did. We didn't even get the door shut before she'd turned into me, and I hugged her. We were taking turns comforting one another, apparently. Well, it's good to take turns.

"Sadie, I hate that man," she said against my shoulder. I didn't say anything. "Every time I see his face, all I can think of is Cameron and how Hughes said that he had it coming. What kind of thing is that to say to a family that just lost someone? They call *us* the monsters?" I knew exactly how she felt, but I let her keep going uninterrupted. She pushed away. Her cheeks were flushed and eyes were red. "And what the hell with the coming down here? It's not enough to call us names on national television? He has to come down here to do it in person?"

I smiled wryly. "We know he's an ass, and that he hates us," I pointed out. "We shouldn't really be surprised when he acts on it."

Madison huffed. "I know, but it still pisses me off. It was hard enough to watch the news, but then to have him dragging up all this shit that I've managed to get past right here in my face. It's more than a person should have to tolerate!"

"If life were fair, I'd agree." I leaned against the edge of my desk, trying to project an air of calm. "We know that life isn't fair, though. We also knew it was going to be a long time before we weren't spending most of our time shoveling shit like this."

"I know," she repeated. "It would be easier to shovel if the shit were from someone else." She paused. "This conversation took a disgusting turn." At least she laughed then, quietly but a laugh, nonetheless. She rubbed her hands over her face and wiped her eyes. "Life goes on, right?"

"Right."

"The woman out there is your animator appointment."

Oh. Well. That made sense. Right, she talks to the dead...

"Send her in."

CHAPTER FIFTEEN

I ended up hiring the woman—Sarah Beaumont was her name—for a trial period.

Things were quiet for a little while, which let me get some paperwork done and reply to some emails, before the phone in the front office rang. Then the phone in my office rang, so I knew it was a call I needed to take.

"Stanton," I answered.

"Hi, Sadie." It was Vance. I sat up straight and bit my lip. My fright response popped up with the idea of an immediate threat, and I felt my fangs descend into my bottom lip. I fought them back again.

"What's wrong?" I asked nervously.

"Well..." I heard him take a deep breath and then let it out in a sigh. "We can't find the Whites."

I blinked. "What? What do you mean you can't find them?"

I could practically hear the helpless shrug. "It's just what I said. We can't find them. It's like they don't exist. We called the number you gave us, but it's been disconnected. And we can't find an Ernest and Regina White anywhere in the area."

"Maybe they weren't local?" I suggested. I got up with the cordless phone to my ear, walking into the front office. I checked around that only Madison was there, and then nodded to the computer. "Can you pull up the Whites?"

"Sure," she said curiously, changing programs and typing in the name.

I leaned over her shoulder and read the screen. "It looks like they gave us a P.O. box in Waterford as an address." Which I gave to him. "They paid the first half of the invoice in cash, and the second was mailed to them at that address. It hasn't been paid yet."

Madison frowned. "I was going to contact them today. What's going on?"

"Good luck with that," I murmured. "Apparently, their number has been disconnected." I straightened and walked back to my office. "I'm sorry. That's all we have on them."

"It gives me something to run down," Vance said almost apologetically. "I'm sure we'll find them. People sometimes just do weird things."

I smiled weakly. "I appreciate your trying to make me feel better," I said.

After a pause, he said, "I saw you on the news."

Sitting down hard in my chair, I put my face in my free hand. "Already?"

"Unfortunately, yes. You did a really good job keeping your cool with that ass around."

"Thanks," I said, half-mumbled into my palm.

I heard another deep breath from his side of the line before he said, "So, Marlowe would probably gut me if she heard me ask this, but do you want to meet up for that coffee tomorrow night?"

Pulling my face from my hand, I smiled a little. "Isn't it against some kind of rules to date a suspect?"

"You're not a *serious* suspect," he said. "So, it's...a gray area."

"Alright then," I said. "Tomorrow night."

☾O☽

It was probably about an hour later that I wandered back into Madison's office.

"Do we have any more appointments?" I asked. Frankly, I'd just had enough of the whole evening and was ready to throw in the towel, call it a day. When she shook her head, I decided on just that. "Come on. We're shutting the office early."

"We're what?" she asked, blinking at me in surprise.

"We're shutting the office early and going on before dawn comes," I said.

She shut off her computer while eyeing me like I was going crazy. Maybe I was, but I thought I also had a right to. "Where are we going?" she asked.

Well, I hadn't gotten that far yet.

I thought for a moment and said, "The beach."

☾O☽

Who expects a vampire to go to the beach, right?

Since every other business was open twenty-four hours now, the beaches were, too. Vampires could go outside just fine. It was sun that was the problem, but the beach at night was covered in moon, and that was lovely.

We closed the office and drove to Niantic. It's a quaint New England village situated right on the shore of Long Island Sound, providing a sort of low-key beach compared to those right up against the ocean proper. We parked the car and then headed out onto the boardwalk, enjoying the dim light and the quiet. There were plenty of others out there, mostly vampires and those who came with them, but nighttime is still just...quieter. It had more appeal than usual that night since I'd had just about as much *loud* as I could take for an evening.

"It's nice to be able to visit the beach without having to hop over locked gates to get here," I commented wryly, thinking about all the decades I'd spent as a vampire in a world where we were just myth and nightmare.

"You being you, I imagine that wasn't something you did often," Madison teased.

I laughed. "You are correct," I said. "I've never been much of a rule-breaker and have only done it when there was no other choice available. Simone would take me on occasion, whenever we found a beach that wasn't locked up. Cameron, however," I laughed again, "would hop the fence."

Madison grinned. "He was a terrible law student," she said. "Breaking all the rules."

"That he was," I agreed. "Though I never really found the beach visits to be big rules to be broken."

She didn't disagree with that.

We passed a guy with a cart selling hotdogs and much to my amusement, Madison stopped to get one. I teased her about the wolf/dog thing for a minute but was then distracted by the smell of it. I kept leaning over to stick my face closer.

"Would you stop that?" she chastised me, but fondly. "It's getting creepy, and your big ole head in the way makes it hard to eat my food."

"I can't help it," I said in a half-whine. "I miss real food."

She swatted at me. "Your liquid diet is not my fault, and I don't need your slobber as a condiment."

I frowned but pulled back. "Vampires don't slobber. We stop creating saliva."

"Don't need the bio lesson," she said around a bite of food. "Just need you away from my food."

"Don't talk with your mouth full." I stuck my tongue out

at her.

We kept walking as she finished her late-night meal, and I kept staring at it enviously. It really wasn't even that I liked hotdogs that much, as a rule. I just missed food that required chewing. It's really odd the things you miss when you become a vampire.

Once she was done, we went up the street to a great used bookstore—or part of it, as there were multiple locations in town—and checked out the horror section for laughs. I'd been given more copies of *Dracula* in my life than I ever knew existed in one region. Still, it was fun to look. Madison bought a cookbook just to bug me, I thought.

We went back out to the beach then and walked in the water for a while. It wasn't warm, this time of the year, but we didn't mind. It was just our feet.

Unfortunately, we lost track of time, and before I knew it, I felt those early tendrils of dawn start creeping down my spine. I realized we'd walked a bit far, too. There was no way we were going to get home before the sun rose. On the upside, being an older vamp, I could stay up longer than the young ones, but it was still a head-long sprint back to the car.

Madison popped the back, and I jumped in. Curling up, she tossed an "emergency" blanket over me. It was meant for any emergency, and this qualified.

I lost consciousness by the time I felt the car hit the highway.

CHAPTER SIXTEEN

I hurt like hell, still curled up in the back of the car, when I woke up the next night. I groaned as I unfolded myself from my origami-like structure and crawled over the backseat to get out through one of the doors. I staggered stiffly into the house, where Madison was sitting at the small table in our 'dining corner' having coffee.

She looked up and smirked at me as I came in.

"Rest well?" she drawled sweetly.

"No," I grumbled.

"Well, you're not burnt to a crisp, so I still call that a success," she pointed out.

I shrugged because I knew she was right, but I really didn't want to give voice to admitting it.

After getting breakfast for myself, I trudged back to the table and sat across from her. Well, more like at a right angle to her because the other two edges of the table were pushed back into the corner so there was room to go from the living room to the kitchen. It was a nice house, but it wasn't a huge one.

"I know the sleeping arrangements weren't great," she said after a few moments, "but getting out of the office helped. So, thanks for that."

For that, I managed a smile. "It helped us both."

She smiled back and then got up, gathering her things and heading for work. I finished my blood, then went to take a shower and change my clothes. I had a date with Mr. Johnston, and I didn't want to show up looking like I'd just slept in the back of a car.

☾O☽

Vance and I met at a place in town called Molly's Diner. It was pretty casual but had the benefit of serving all sorts of the city's preternatural. I'd already had breakfast so I wasn't going to have anything now. No matter how chill someone may think they are, watching a vampire drink a glass of A-positive can still be unhinging, and I chose to spare him.

If he stuck around, well, we'd see.

"Tiger," he said, responding to my question.

"I knew you were some kinda cat," I chuckled. "But cats all smell the same to a vampire. No offense."

"None taken." He smiled and sipped his coffee. "All dogs can smell the same to me, but I don't think I'm gonna say that to your secretary."

"I wouldn't."

Setting away his coffee cup, he folded his arms across the edge of the table and looked thoughtful. I got the feeling he was working out what to say next, so I didn't jump in and just let him get there on his own. Although patience hasn't always been one of my specific virtues, being a vampire, in general, often taught you a lot about it.

"You know, I'm really a pretty boring guy," he finally said with a laugh. He had a nice smile and a nice laugh. "I don't have a hundred years of history to talk about like you do. I had a happy childhood. My parents are still alive. I was born in St Louis, went to college in Georgia on a football scholarship, and then moved up here after I became a cop."

"Why did you move up here?" I asked curiously. They had cops down South, I was pretty sure.

He shrugged his broad shoulders. "A combination of things, I guess. A need to just get out of the nest, be on my own, and then a bad breakup." He looked into his cup for a moment. "She was human. Always risky. She found out and thought I was a freak. She tried telling our friends, but they thought she was nuts, and that just made her more mad at me."

I winced. "That's tough," I said sympathetically. "Of course, now..."

Vance chuckled, but it was bitter. "Yeah, now, she's probably in LOHAV."

The reminder of that particular hate group was always enough to make me grimace. He was probably right, though. I'd known a fair few people who'd had others learn about their true natures, whether by accident or confession, and the reactions were a mixed bag. There was the "that's so cool" reaction and then the...chase you around with a pitchfork and torch reaction. Or the "call the sanitarium" people.

And, on rare occasion, came the "me too!"

That was me and Cameron, though we'd recognized each other for what we were pretty quickly. You could smell it.

"I'm sorry to hear it went that way," I said honestly.

"Me too," he agreed. "But hey, it got me up here. I saw the job and applied, they liked my experience, so I packed up my car and moved. I like it up here."

"Even the winters?" I grinned, knowing how different that particular season was between the top and bottom halves of the country.

"Especially the winters," he replied. "I snowboard."

"Nice," I said. "Going out for long periods in the winter can be iffy for vampires, but there's ways. I've even gone skiing a time or two myself. Not that I'm any good at it..."

He laughed. "I thought becoming a vampire made you

good at everything," he teased.

"If only…"

I'd let myself enjoy things a bit too much and forgot what was going on outside the diner, and it was all about to come crashing down.

CHAPTER SEVENTEEN

The door to the diner opened, but I didn't pay it any mind until I saw Vance look over my shoulder. He frowned, and his dark brows drew tight together, which made me turn to see who had walked in.

It was Detective Marlowe, and she looked pissed.

She marched right up to our table and glared daggers at Vance. "*You* shouldn't be here," she hissed. Before he could respond, she snapped her attention to me. "Sadie Stanton, I'm arresting you on suspicion of murder."

"What the—" Vance began angrily, standing up so fast he bumped the table and knocked over the glassware. "Yesterday, we agreed that—"

"Well, it isn't yesterday now, is it?" Nykk snapped back. "We have a werehawk corpse in the morgue with another note and a vampire bite. Two people attacked this woman and both are now dead-by-vampire. She is a vampire. She's under arrest."

⟪O⟫

I sat at a small table in a small room with handcuffs on my wrists. They were inscribed with symbols to keep me from breaking them, which I would have been able to do otherwise with my vampire's strength. Although, I wouldn't have anyway.

Marlowe and Vance sat on the other side of the table, although she'd made it very, very clear that *he* would not be asking any questions. He probably wouldn't even be allowed to speak. I think if she'd had her way, he wouldn't even be allowed in the room, but he was there, anyways, and looking really uncomfortable.

Well, he wasn't the only one.

"Do you recognize this man?" Marlowe asked, putting another picture of a corpse on the table.

I looked at the picture and sighed. "Yes. He attacked me at the Coven House."

She nodded and took the picture back. "What do you know about him?"

"Nothing else, really," I replied with a shrug. "He was a shifter, some kind of bird, but that's about it. He wasn't a great fighter."

"He had a note in his pocket with the date, time, and location to match your attack at the Coven House," Marlowe went on.

"So, after the first attempt didn't kill me, they sent this guy," I muttered.

"Who are 'they,' Miss Stanton?"

"Fuck if I know," I replied before I could stop myself. "I don't know who has this big of a grudge against me." Well, there was Hughes, but I didn't think he'd go as far as to hire people to attack me. I guess I couldn't be sure, but...it was still hard to wrap my brain around. "I'm not the only vampire in town, you know."

Marlowe didn't look impressed with my attitude. "It's in your best interest to cooperate, Miss Stanton."

Her tone made my fangs descend, but I pressed my lips shut and willed them back.

"I'm doing my best," I said tightly, "but I'm pretty strung out right now. I didn't kill anyone."

"Don't you find it a strange coincidence that two people who attacked you are now both dead?" Marlowe asked.

"Of course I do," I replied, lifting both hands to rub my face since it was both or nothing. "But they were sent after me, so there's a third person in the works here. I think I could be, you know, being set up!"

"Why would someone want to set you up?"

I dropped my hands back to the table and my head followed. I could do just fine in front of reporters but, apparently, cops were too much. "I don't know that any more than I know why someone would want to kill me."

Marlowe made a noncommittal sort of noise.

Blowing out a breath, I sat up again and leaned back in my chair as best I could. There was no getting comfortable, though, so I didn't even bother trying. "Do you have any proof that it was me or just that it was a vampire?" I frowned. "Do you even know if it was a vampire or just someone making it look like that? We kinda have a distinctive MO, but I can't think of anyone dumb enough to make it so obvious."

"In moments of high emotion, people tend to do dumb things and resort to their basic natures."

I frowned. "Is that a racist stab?"

"This isn't going to help you," Vance murmured, but Marlowe silenced him with a look.

"We have confirmed that a vampire killed the first victim, and we expect the same result for the second."

Well, damn. "What about DNA?" Then I winced. Right.

"You know there won't be any DNA in the bites."

Vampires didn't have saliva.

I was going to be damned by a lack of evidence rather than evidence?

Everything started getting really hazy right about then. I remember being asked questions about my alibis.

Apparently, they were both killed at night, so daylight was no defense. It seemed to happen at times I was home alone or on my way home, where I'd be alone for a while until Madison got home. Locations were close…

It was all circumstantial, but damning, nonetheless.

When they were done, I was put into a cell.

Chapter Eighteen

On the upside, I was allowed visitors. It kinda wasn't totally an upside, but it seemed better than being in solitary.

"Oh, Sadie," Madison said, crying as soon as she got to the bars. She reached up to put her hands on them but stopped immediately, because she could sense there was silver in them and it would burn her. For a moment, I thought she'd do it anyway, just to move closer, but she didn't, and I was glad. I didn't need her getting hurt.

"I'm sure we'll get this sorted out," I said with more confidence than I felt. "I know it looks bad, like, really bad, but it's just a mix-up."

She didn't look like she believed it any more than I did.

"They think you murdered people!"

"Marlowe thinks I did," I muttered. "And I'll admit that I can see her logic, but I know I didn't kill anyone, so that will come out. They'll find the real killer, and it will be fine. I'll get out of here." I gestured up and around. "And no windows, so they aren't going to let me fry ahead of time. Nothing to worry about."

She sniffled and blew out a breath. "I don't see how you can say that."

Before either of us said anything else, a uniformed officer stepped in. "You have another visitor," she said.

"I'm more popular in prison than out of it, apparently," I quipped morbidly.

A moment later, I was surprised to see Dakota walking in. She looked amused as she took in my situation.

"What are you doing here?" I asked in surprise.

"You think you'd be nicer. You need all the friends you can get," she returned without missing a beat.

My brows shot up. "Are we friends now?"

She looked like she was thinking about this. "We're not enemies."

I guess that was true. "I still didn't expect you to visit me."

"I had an hour free," she said. "I wanted to see what the real situation was. I know you didn't kill anyone. I know killers, and you are not one, so someone has fucked something up royally. I wouldn't be surprise if some LOHAV twit was behind this."

"I wouldn't be surprised, either," Madison mumbled.

Dakota looked at her like she'd only just noticed her. "Oh, right. The secretary. I'm Dakota."

Madison forced a smile. "I know. Stop sneaking into the office, would you? Give a girl a heart attack."

The strange woman's brow arched. "You seem pretty fit to me."

My practically-a-sister blinked, and then blushed slightly, looking away. Did this hunter lady just hit on her? I wasn't sure, but this didn't seem like the time or the place. I cleared my throat, and Dakota turned her attention lazily back toward me.

"Hughes has been trying to get in here to have a go at you," she announced, deadpan as ever. "You'll be happy to know your boyfriend—"

"I don't have a boyfriend."

"—whatever. Your boyfriend is blockading him. My money's on the cop, but if you hear the howling, that would be it."

That was just what I needed, wasn't it.

☾○☽

Dawn came not long after they left, and at least I didn't have to endure anything for the next several hours. Some more bad dreams as I was coming back to life, of course, but they weren't anything compared to what I woke up to. Sleeping in the cell on that cot was far worse than sleeping in the back of the car.

It was only going to get better.

As I sat up and stretched out my very sore body, I saw the door to my little block of cells open just ahead of a terrible racket. I frowned as I listened to the screaming and thrashing, the sounds of something big—like a body—throwing itself against walls and doors and other bodies. They were bringing in some sort of maniac, apparently, and I knew it was a preternatural maniac because of the fact that this was the supernatural cellblock.

Dakota was the face I saw again, but this time, she was on one side of the aforementioned thrashing body while Vance took the other. Between their matching six-foot, muscled forms and preternatural strength, they were the best equipped to handle whatever that was…

They were having a hell of a time, though, and between that and the smell, I figured out it was a vampire.

A psychotic vampire.

They reached the first empty cell and forcibly *threw* him inside. The two of them together barely managed to get the cell door shut before he was throwing himself at the gate. I heard the sizzling of flesh as the vampire grabbed onto the silver bar, shrieking in pain but not letting go, while a gloved Vance shut the door.

Vance looked at Dakota, then looked at me, and left without a word.

"Great. A roommate," I said with a grimace.

"This vampire hurt a human this morning," she told me. "I was tasked to find him, and this one, I actually found. There's…lots wrong with him."

"So I see," I said.

She blew out a breath and walked over to my cell. "Rumor is they're hauling you out of here for arraignment shortly, now that you're living again."

I made a face. "Lucky me. Because being arraigned on murder charges was definitely on my list of things to do before I die for good." I leaned back against the cell wall, the only wall that wasn't a line of bars that would burn the hell out of me.

"I can't believe this wasn't on your to-do list for the night," she drawled.

"Are you here just to bother me?" I asked tiredly. "I mean, I really try to not be this snarky, especially with people I really only barely know, but I'm kind of having a bad day here."

She looked at me in silence for just long enough to be unnerving, then she smirked, tilted her head, and walked out.

☾O☽

She had been right, though. I was brought out for arraignment. They had to drive me to New London for that, since that was the seat of the county.

I pled not guilty. Of course.

Bail was set at *one million dollars.*

I nearly died for good right then and there.

☾O☽

The trip out of the courthouse and back to the Adelheid jail was just another sequence of haziness. I noticed, vaguely, that I was taken through the back door. I kind of wondered about that but not too much, because I had other things on my mind. About a million of them.

I stretched out on the cot, figuring I would be here until the cops figured out it wasn't me.

I wasn't sure how long that would be.

As it happened, I didn't wait that long. Well, to get out of the cell. The cops still thought I'd done it. But the same uniform from before came and walked me out of the cell and to the desk, where I found Dakota...again.

"Do you live here now?" I asked with a half-smile. "If you do, maybe you have some idea of what's going on."

"No, but yes." She turned to the desk and signed something on a clipboard.

"What?" I felt dumb.

She turned back to me. The cop behind the counter nodded, and the one who had walked me out took off the cuffs. I felt more and more confused.

"I don't live here," Dakota said, "but I know what's going on. Your bail has been posted."

"What?" I said again, even dumber now.

She seemed to be thinking that about me as well. "I can have them put you back in the cell, if you'd rather."

I blinked. "No! No. That's fine."

The cops just nodded at us and left without saying a word, something like underpaid extras in some cop movie. Dakota nodded for me to walk with her, and I did. Just a few steps away, Vance was waiting for us.

"Press is still mobbing outside," he said. "Hughes is

whipping them up into a lather, but the back is still clear. Come on." He nodded and walked with us to the back, opening the door and looking outside. Once he felt sure it was clear, he gestured for us to go. He took my hand as I passed and squeezed it, then sent us off.

Dakota's car was parked there. At least, I figured it was her car because she had the keys and we got into it.

"Are you going to tell me what's going on now?" I asked as she pulled out of the back lot of the station and onto the back roads.

"I thought that was obvious." She looked at me and saw I wasn't following, so she sighed dramatically. "I posted bail for you, so now you're my responsibility."

I stared at her. "You posted bail?"

"Yes. Where is the complexity in this statement?"

"Bond would have been, like, a hundred grand!"

"Yeah? So?"

"You have a hundred grand just laying around to bail out some woman you barely know?" I all but shouted in my surprise.

"And people say *I'm* rude," she said as she kept driving along the dark roads, away from the police and away from the press. "Just try not to do anything stupid, okay? Until we get this shit cleared up, you're my problem before anyone else's. And if you run, then you're my problem, only then I'll also be pissed off."

Chapter Nineteen

Straight from the station, Dakota took me to a hotel. About fifty jokes sprang to mind, all of them more suited for a twelve-year-old boy than a vampire of my age.

We walked into the lobby of the Adelheid Inn, as it was so creatively called, and Dakota stalked—I don't think she ever just walked anywhere—up to the desk. I lingered back since I knew nothing about what was going on. After a moment, she returned. Well, sort of. It was more like a slow banking maneuver with a close pass, nodding at me to follow. I returned to my inner twelve-year-old and considered just ignoring her till she spoke to me like a person, but then I remembered the magic word.

Bail.

I bowed my head in shame and followed.

The Adelheid Inn was popular among the visiting vampire set for its full array of inner rooms with no windows at all. These had been a detriment in the past with primarily human clientele and their silly need for sunlight, but now, business was booming, and I was part of the parade.

Dakota led me to a room inside on the second floor, unlocking the door with an old-fashioned key and letting me in.

This was when I decided to ask.

"I hope this doesn't sound ungrateful or something, but I'm kinda curious... Why are we here?" I stopped at the bed and turned to face her. "Why can't I just go home?"

She met my gaze with a look that had 'oh, you poor dumb kid' all over it. "The press has your house surrounded. There's blood in the water, and the sharks are out."

I dropped my head back and groaned at the ceiling, then collapsed on the bed. "This sucks."

"Adequate summary of the situation," she declared. "I'm gonna go to your place and get you some stuff. I'll see if that wolf of yours can help."

"How are you going to get in there without being mobbed by the sharks?" I asked without looking at her.

She snorted. Was it a laugh? I wasn't sure. "I'm a woman of many talents. Sit tight. Don't order too much on room service or I'll make you pay for it yourself."

That was all she said before she was gone.

I was left alone with my thoughts...

...which was precisely the last thing I wanted to be.

How the hell had this happened? How was I being charged with murder? Arrested! Out on bail! I never imagined I'd end up here, and certainly not for something I didn't do. There had been more than a few anti-preternatural protesters I'd wanted to put in the dirt, but I hadn't done it. Now, I almost wished I had, because then I'd understand why I was enduring this shit.

Sitting up, I looked around for the remote and turned the TV on.

I skipped past a couple of channels playing the news, and I went past those as fast as I could press the buttons. *Dracula* was playing on another station, but I jumped past that, too. I finally settled on some sort of reality TV cooking show. I might not have been able to eat that sort of thing anymore, but it was still kind of fun to watch people making it. I could sort of vicariously live through others.

Madison always said it was creepy the way I watched

her eat steak.

The television made decent background noise to try to help me drone out my thoughts so I didn't keep running in futile circles, but it made me think about a lot of foods I couldn't eat.

I was knee-deep in thoughts about beef wellington and chateaubriand when the door handle shook.

Rationally, I told myself that it was Dakota coming back, but I still sat up straight and felt my fangs descend in that defense reaction. I held my body very still, watching the door as it swung open.

A blonde blur streaked across the room, and the only thing that kept me from panicking was my ability to recognize the voice shrieking my name. I now had to brace myself for another reason—a different sort of attack—but I still only barely kept myself on the bed as Madison collided with me.

"Sadie! I was so worried!" she exclaimed as she hugged me.

I hugged her back. "It's okay," I said, patting her shoulder. I had to say it a few more times before she finally let me go, sniffling and wiping her face.

"Dakota came by the office to ask me about getting your things, and I made her tell me where you were," she went on. "She wasn't going to. Keeping you all secret and stuff."

"But she can be very persistent," Dakota drawled as she walked in with a backpack over one shoulder. She shut the door behind her and threw the bag in the chair in the corner. "I know when I'm beat."

"I haven't known you long, but that somehow surprises me," I returned dryly, then I looked at Madison again. I brushed some of her hair off her forehead with a sympathetic smile. "I know this is all pretty shocking, but it'll be alright. We'll get it sorted out."

She nodded a little.

I took a breath so I could sigh. "Where are you going to stay? I hear the house isn't a good place to go."

"So I hear, too," she agreed wanly. "I'm staying with one of the pack girls. She has a spare room and a brother big enough to lift any press person overhead. Besides, us wolves—pack or not—kinda need to stick together."

"Is it getting that bad?" I asked with a frown.

"I'm afraid it's looking that way," Madison said wearily. If she had been in wolf form, her ears and tail would have been drooping. "Gabe says that some of the wolves are talking about retaliation against the vampires."

I groaned and pressed the heels of my hands to my temples. Yeah, that was just what we all needed right then.

"I'm sorry," Madison sighed. "I know you don't need more stress right now."

"It's okay," I said, patting her arm. "We'll get it sorted. I may put a call in to Gabe myself and see if I can help." I looked up at Dakota, who was casually leaning against the wall and waiting for...something. "Can I do that or am I in the witness protection program?"

"You can make a call," she returned.

The stress was getting to me, though, and inwardly, I chastised myself to watch my attitude. I was out of prison because of the Amazon of a woman over there.

I turned back to Madison and saw she had dark circles beneath her red eyes, and she looked pretty ragged. "Go to your friend's house and get some rest, Madison. Sunrise is coming soon, and I'm about to become terrible company." I half-smiled as encouragingly as I could.

She nodded and hugged me again, so tight that if I needed to breathe, it would've been a problem. Then she wiped her face, thanked Dakota, and hurried out.

I was left alone with Dakota, and I wasn't sure if that was better or worse than being alone. I looked at her. She looked back at me.

"I have a message from your boyfriend," she finally said. When I looked confused, she added, "The cop."

"He's still not my boyfriend," I said quickly. Hadn't we done this already?

She arched her brow. "Well, tell *him* that. It's terrible to see a grown man mope."

That was...weird and sweet all at the same time, I thought. "Uh, what...what's the message?" I asked, trying to not think about the weird feeling I had going on.

"He said he'll call you after sunset. Don't call him, though, because it could look bad," she went on. She pushed off the wall and grabbed the backpack, walking it over to the bed and dropping it beside me. "I'm out again. I got my cell. Number is in the bag."

With that, she left again without another word.

CHAPTER TWENTY

Before I went to sleep that morning, I called Gabe. Unfortunately for me, the conversation consisted mostly of my talking and him saying "I know, I know, Sadie. I'm working on it."

I went to bed that morning feeling more discouraged than I could remember feeling for a really long time.

❨O❩

That day, I dreamed about the war. The second Great War. Back then, Simone and I had worked in European hospitals while bombs fell. We took every night shift and worked feverishly to disappear before day came.

I remembered asking her once if it wouldn't just be easier if people knew what we were. That was not an idea she was happy about. In fact, I couldn't remember her ever being angrier at me.

Simone and I had always gotten along really well ever since she turned me. I couldn't understand why she had gotten *so* furious when I brought this up. She said our secrecy was paramount. It was the most important thing we had. We were vampires, for fuck's sake, we had to keep hidden. We couldn't bring ourselves out into the light.

I remembered later, when the trials for legality began, that I thought a lot about that night. I hadn't thought about it for the past year, though. Ever since things changed. I mean, yeah, things were tough, but they weren't *that* bad. Okay, they *could* be that bad at times, but for the most part, I thought legality had been a good. Living outside of the shadows had been such a relief.

I still couldn't understand, even all these decades later, why she couldn't see that possibility way back then.

But anyway, that was what I dreamed of that day. When I woke up, I wasn't feeling any better than I had when I went into my daylight coma.

☾O☽

I'd been up and about for maybe forty minutes when Dakota came in.

She didn't knock or announce herself in any way, but I was somehow not at all surprised. I just settled back into the sofa and watched her stalk to the small dresser with the complementary bottles of water. She grabbed one and drank the whole thing before turning to me.

"It's gotten worse."

I raised my brows and was suddenly hungry. An uncommon but not unheard of stress reaction in a vampire. We were all human once, after all. "How?" I was learning to not mince words with this one.

She put the bottle back on the counter. "Do you recall that very cheerful fella tossed in the cell while you were there?" I just answered with a nod. "He's dead."

At this, my brows went from raised to knit. "What happened?"

"He went into his daylight coma and didn't wake up again. He was taken to the hospital, where they confirmed that the animation process was dead. He wasn't coming back. They shipped him off to the medical examiner."

I leaned my head back against the couch and closed my eyes, rubbing them with the heels of my hand. "I don't suppose there's any word yet?"

"Not yet. Technically, I'm not supposed to be telling you any of this, but I don't really care." She shrugged with such lack of fucks that it was an audible gesture. "His first-glance report said it had the appearance of natural causes—"

"Vampires don't have natural causes. We don't die in our sleep," I interrupted her.

She growled and it sounded a lot like an angry cat. "I'm aware of this," she said, voice pitched low with annoyance. "You asked if there was word and I'm telling you what those words were."

"Sorry."

She grunted and went on. "He's comparing the brains right now. Last I heard, he was seeing signs of similarities but wasn't ready to say anything for sure.

"He also told me," she went on after a moment, "that after the first vampire autopsy, he ordered some regular living vamps to get their brain scanned or whatever so he could compare them all. He's working on that now, too."

"That's a good idea," I said. My hands were still over my eyes because I was clearly three years old. If I couldn't see a problem, then the problem couldn't see me! "Anything else go to hell while I was unconscious?"

I didn't like how long she was taking to answer, so I peeled away one hand and opened that eye to look at her. She was looking back at me in an unnervingly steady way.

"Not really," she finally said, and I rolled my eyes at the adrenaline she'd resurrected in me.

Before I could yell at her for that, her phone rang. She answered it with a terse, "Dakota. Go." She listened for a moment, and then handed it to me. "It's your boyfriend."

The phone was in my hand before I could retort. "Hi,

Vance. Aren't you going to get in trouble for this?"

"Not since they think I'm talking to Dakota, if anyone bothers to check," he replied. "How are you holding up?"

Lousy.

Terrible.

Frightened.

Tired.

"Fine," I replied. "How're you?"

He laughed a little at, I assumed, the banality of the exchange before saying, "Fine. I have some news. Wright has compared all the different vamp brains, the healthy ones and then the dead-dead ones. He says there is a definite sickness of some sort in the two dead ones. He's working on theories about how that's possible in a disease-resistant species, but it's something that fucked up their brains pretty good. And it looks like it's what finally killed him for good."

I boggled at what could possibly do that while we said good-bye and hung up.

"So, basically," Dakota began after I relayed what Vance had just told me, "what we're saying here is that we still have two bat-shit crazy vampires running around with apparent needs to attack people without provocation."

"Yeah. Basically."

She snorted. "Well, ain't that fucking fantastic?"

CHAPTER TWENTY-ONE

We drove to the Coven House.

Basically, if you had a problem with vampires, going to one of the 'hot spots' of vampire life was a good way to go, and when we called, she said we could. Few people just showed up unannounced on Jade.

The unreasonably imposing Dakota was met at the door by the unreasonably imposing Warden Shayna, but we were escorted straight in and to the 'fancy' sitting room since we were expected. We sat down and waited for Jade, which wasn't very long before she came in.

"Terrible times," she said simply, cutting right to the chase as she took a seat in a brocade armchair that nearly swallowed her. "What can I do? I've already spoken with the police. I'm afraid I did not have much to give them."

"Well," I began, debating how much I should share and how much I was probably allowed to share. "We know now the vampires who have been attacking people are sick somehow." Her mouth opened, and I held up a hand. "We haven't figured out how that's possible yet, but it's happened. They are basically crazy, and they are dying from it."

She nodded slowly. Her face was generally a porcelain, impenetrable mask, but I thought I saw some sorrow in her very dark eyes. "You have come here, then, hoping for insight on what an insane, dying vampire might do?"

Dakota and I exchanged a look. "I guess. Yeah. Basically."

The corners of her perfectly-painted lips lifted slightly. "They will want to go home," she said simply.

"Home?" I repeated. I thought about it, and about myself, and I supposed that it made sense.

Jade inclined her head in a sort of nod. She opened her mouth to speak, but there was a different voice instead.

From behind Jade's over-sized chair came the too-thin, too-pale, too-small form of Abby. She was a vampire, old and young all at once, and quite complex besides. She was sucking from a hospital blood-bag like it was a cold soda from the convenience store.

"It's not going to just be where they lived," she pointed out, moving around to sit on the couch with us without being invited. Even Jade didn't speak out about that, though, because Abby was...something else. "When a vampire loses their mind, it's like they become...primitive. It's primal. It's what feels like home to them. Where they feel safe. Where they want to be. That might be their current address, but with a vampire? Often not."

"She's right," Jade agreed. Although she might not say something about it, she did give the small vampire A Look that no one missed. "We have to determine where these vampires might feel at home and thus would go to."

"I don't know either of them at all," I said with a hint of despair.

Jade sighed softly. "One of them is a coven vampire," she said. "Her, I knew. Sweet girl. She hasn't been a vampire all that long, really. She has been living here since she turned, but she was at her parents' home on the outskirts of town. I think she would go there."

Dakota was already on her feet and heading for the door without a word.

"I guess she's checking that out," I deadpanned.

"What about the other?" I asked Jade.

She could only shake her head. "The police asked me, but I did not recognize him, I'm afraid. I am sorry."

I managed a small smile. "It's okay. You've been a big help." I got to my feet and got ready to leave as well before I looked at the door and dropped my head with a sigh.

"What is it, Sadie?" Jade asked with concern.

"She was my ride."

❨O❩

I ended up walking. The color and intensity of my language grew the further I went, but at least being a vampire meant I didn't get tired in the same way humans did. Our fatigue was either blood loss or mental.

I was mentally tired, but my body could go on forever.

Hopefully, it would.

Using my phone, I pulled up what little information the internet had to offer about this fourth vampire. I checked his last-known address and a workplace I found on his social media, but none of them gave me any success. I scrolled through the photos he had public and tried to piece together where some of them may be taken, if they were local. I found two that fit that bill and checked them both.

No luck. Anyone I asked hadn't seen him in days.

I was just heading back to the hotel when Dakota called me.

"I found her," she said simply. "Already dead."

"Damn," I sighed. "I've been trying to find the other one, but no luck there—"

"He's already been found," she cut me off.

I stared at my phone with annoyance. "What?"

I swore I could hear her shrugging. "He's already been found and his body was called in. Also dead. Wright is getting onto the autopsies right away and said I could watch. You can't, but you can sit in my car with your phone on."

☾O☽

This sucked.

Dakota parked her car in the guest parking lot of the OCME satellite office. She called me when she reached the right floor and just held her phone while she talked with Wright and he did his ME thing.

"You'd think that carving through a vampire skull would be easier than a human's." This was Wright. "On account of how long they have been, yes?" There was a muffled sound of impatient agreement from the hunter. "Well, it's not. See, something about the magic that animates them also makes them hardier. The bones actually become harder, and—" Anything more he had to say about vampire anatomy was drowned out by the high-pitched whirring of the bone saw.

This part, I was able to envision all too clearly, and I grimaced, even if I wasn't actually seeing anything.

"That looks like shit, Doc," Dakota said. Scientific, that one.

"It is a very unhealthy brain," Wright agreed. There were some shuffling noises. "Visual inspection puts it in line with the other three, I'm afraid."

Okay, no shock there.

"I don't suppose these brains give us any clue about what has done this to them." Dakota.

"Not them specifically. Not yet. But I may have something."

I sat up straight, suddenly straining to hear even though the call quality was pretty good, as was my vampire hearing.

"When I started the first autopsy, something about it

was familiar." Shuffling of papers. "It took me until just a bit ago to pinpoint it." More shuffling, but not like loose papers. Flipping through a book or magazine? "Here." Silence.

Several moments of silence and me working hard to keep myself from screaming at someone to speak.

Then Dakota said, "This fucker invented a vampire virus?!"

Well. There it was.

"A theoretical virus, yes. However, everything he says there seems to match what I see here."

"Can I borrow this?"

☾O☽

Five minutes later, Dakota threw herself into the driver's seat beside me. "I'm dropping you back off at the hotel." She threw the magazine into my lap.

"What? Why?" I asked, lifting the magazine and looking for the article.

"I have someone to find."

When I got to the article in question, my eyes nearly bulged out of my head when I saw just *who* had written it.

Walter Warren.

Chapter Twenty-Two

There are never really any coincidences, I supposed.

The woman who was worried about her brother apparently had good reason to be worried. Her idiot sibling had come up with a way to make a vampire virus, published it with his name, and then actually *did* it! This guy would have every vampire on the planet gunning for him once they found out.

Dakota just had to find him first.

Who knew how many other vampires were out there sick? If one of them killed him, he couldn't help us stop the damage or find out who they were.

My problem, however, was that just sitting here was going to drive me bonkers. I couldn't just sit and do nothing with all of this going on and these dark shadows looming over my head. So, I started to think. And think. And think...

And think.

I was beginning to fear that my own brain would melt.

How was a virus given to vampires transmitted? It wasn't by air, because our breathing was intermittent. You couldn't rely on that. And we stopped secreting things from our skin, so no touch-contamination. We didn't develop mucus, so no sneezes or coughs.

What did that leave?

Food-borne illness.

Blood.

Butcher.

I snapped my fingers and jumped to my feet, then stopped. I had something else in my brain. It was a small thought, sitting over in the corner. Small, but loud. It wanted me to remember something...

That first vampire.

The image of his truly-dead face flashed before my eyes, because now I knew why he looked familiar.

I had seen him coming out of the butcher's shop.

☾O☽

I probably shouldn't have been doing exactly what I was doing. If I had been a smart vampire, I would have called Vance. Or called Dakota or Madison to call him. I would have passed along this information to the proper authorities— those not on bail for murder—to follow up.

But I just knew this was all connected. No coincidences, remember? If I could help solve this, then it would cascade. I just *knew* it. It would help these vampires, it would help the community, it would get them off each other's backs and away from their throats, and somewhere in that mess would be the key to get *me* off the hook.

I walked into the butcher's shop.

Unlike the last time, I knew the woman behind the counter. She flashed me a big smile, and perhaps I was lucky and she hadn't seen any of the news.

Then again, I was just a vampire looking for some groceries, right? Nothing wrong with that.

"Hey, Lisa," I said with a smile. "How's business?"

"About the usual," she said. "Gotta say the vampire trade has gone a long way for me." She owned the shop along with her long-time partner Vicky.

I chuckled. I was forcing it, I knew, but I hoped she couldn't tell. "Hey, we do what we can for local business," I said. I then put on a 'curious' expression, which was less forced than the chuckle really. "Hey, I was in here the other day, and you had a new guy working here. Didn't realize you were hiring."

"Yeah, we needed someone part-time to cover the night shifts, and he seemed like a real hard worker," Lisa replied with a frown and shake of her head.

"But?" I prompted, trying to not sound over-eager.

"But he only worked those couple of days, and now nothing. I haven't heard word one."

Well, that was interesting.

My brain raced. I thought it might go so fast it just left my head, but it stayed in place and smoked its tires. A new guy, sounds great enough to hire and then only works for a couple of days—a couple of days where vampires get mysteriously ill—then he vanishes.

Coincidence?

I needed to talk to him.

"Lisa..." I began. "I have to ask you something, and I know you're not going to like it."

❨O❩

Never be too proud to beg and spill your guts on the floor.

It had taken some convincing for Lisa to bend her privacy policies, but she had known me for a long time and told herself I was just helping check on his safety. Which maybe I was. He'd be safer in jail if wind of this ever got out.

Okay, I didn't have any proof that he was involved, but it was just too convenient.

I had to call a cab to bring me to the guy's house, which

was little more than a trailer parked on the opposite side of town. I asked the guy to wait for me as I got out and walked up to the front door.

I knocked, but there was no answer. I knocked again, but it was to the same result.

Frowning, I debated if I wanted to add breaking and entering to my charges. After all, it couldn't be much worse than murder, right?

Except this time, I'd have actually done it.

I chose to go around to the back and see if there were any clues there.

I did.

There was.

There was a body.

CHAPTER TWENTY-THREE

This was bad. This was really bad.

I stared at the body and the bitemarks on the neck. The blood from them was dried, so it wasn't very recent. There was a piece of paper stuck to his chest.

Inching closer, I read what was there and got as far as 'To Sadie' before I ripped it off and hurried back to the taxi. I tried to look calm, but I can't imagine I succeeded. I stuffed the paper into my pocket as I got in and asked him to take me to the hotel, where I paid him and hurried to the room.

Fortunately, I wasn't capable of hyperventilating, but my brain felt like someone had lit it on fire.

I knew I needed to let the police know there was a body there, but I couldn't call them myself. I tried calling Madison instead. As the phone rang, I tried not to think about all the ways that body could be tied to me—my cab ride there, the vampire bite—and how I had just tampered with a crime scene.

Given that Madison didn't answer, though, I had plenty of time to think about it all anyway.

I hung up and tried her cell phone, but also no answer. She was probably in the bathroom—having a need to do that and all—so I just sent her a text for when she got out, and I went back to my wallowing. I'd give myself a few moments to calm down, and then I'd call Dakota.

While I was doing that, though, I pulled the note out of

my pocket.

To Sadie.

You always were so smart. Do you remember Atlantic City? I have your puppy. Come find me.

Simone

I sat down. I didn't even consider I wasn't anywhere near a piece of furniture, so I just hit the floor instead. I barely noticed, though. All I could do was watch my mind race away without me.

Simone... Simone. My Simone? How could it be?

I could feel all the psychological triggers for tears, and my body exhibited some of the physical symptoms without the actual waterworks. Ice had formed directly in the center of my body, and I thought I would throw up if I could.

Simone...

Had she done all this? Had she framed me? But what did she have to do with the virus and the sick vampires? But... But... But...

Coincidences. It was all just too many of them. It had to be interconnected, like the web of some terrible, poisonous spider that wanted to see me dangle and then die.

But why would Simone want that?

❰O❱

It took a while for the haze to clear from my mind. Once it did, I was able to convince myself that I could not figure out *why* until I knew *where*.

I looked at the note again. It was obviously taunting me, and it wanted me to find her. What were the clues?

Atlantic City.

Puppy?

I remembered Atlantic City. We were there not long before I decided to go on my way. It was quite a sight, really, but we didn't spend much time in the usual haunts, as it were. It was one of the places I liked going to the beach at night, and she always went with me.

Pain wracked my brain and my heart again as I thought about our strolls down the boardwalk and through the sand. We didn't have a dog, though. I didn't have one now. I'd never had a... Wolf.

Werewolf.

Madison.

My panicked haze resumed as I tried to keep my terror from overwhelming me. She had Madison. She had taken Madison. I tried calling my near-sister again anyway, but again, no answer. The text hadn't been read either.

That bitch had Madison!

Those were the words that just kept circulating through my brain.

Atlantic city. Boardwalk. Beach. Sand. Niantic! I went there with Madison just a few nights ago.

Had Simone been watching?

I ran out of the hotel so fast the employees probably didn't even see me.

☾O☽

There's nothing like having to take a cab to a rescue mission, but I felt sure Simone wouldn't do anything to Madison until I was there. This was, for some reason, about hurting *me*. I had to be there to witness it for it to hurt the most.

That didn't keep me from being impatient. I tried to not

annoy my cab driver so he didn't drop me off halfway there, but it was a serious struggle. I tapped one foot and shook the other nervously, staring out the window as the scenery didn't pass by nearly fast enough.

He dropped me off in front of some restaurant on the main road downtown, and I rushed off onto the beach after just throwing money behind me.

Once on the sand, I stopped. I closed my eyes and took a long, deep breath through my nose. I picked up on all the smells of the beach. The salty ocean air. The sand. The people who had been here during the day. The food being cooked in the restaurant. So many things. I struggled to pick through them. I needed wolf. But there had been a lot of dogs here lately.

I finally caught the faintest trace of wolf. There was more to it. Sweat. Fear.

Like a supernatural bloodhound, I followed that scent. I didn't even bother opening my eyes, I just followed blind. The sound of a heartbeat cut through the night, and I recognized the beat as too rapid to be normal. It was the heartbeat of someone who was afraid or angry.

As the scent grew stronger, and the sound grew louder, I opened my eyes and discovered myself in a very dark corner of the beach. My vision could pierce through it easily, however, and I saw Simone. She sat on a large rock in front of the wooden boardwalk, with a thin silver chain in her gloved hand, the other end wrapped around Madison's neck. The werewolf was on her knees and holding her body very still. The chain was looped in such a way that if she moved at all, it would burn her.

I could see the tears in her eyes. I felt my own rage surge, but I forced myself to approach calmly.

There was someone else there. A small, geeky-looking man in glasses. He was tied up too, but he was human so just plain rope was fine. Pieces fell through my mind like a puzzle dumped out but falling into the right places. That had to be Warren.

It all fit together now.

My eyes found Simone's, and she smiled, but it was sad. "You always were so smart."

CHAPTER TWENTY-FOUR

Seeing her was like a stake straight through my non-beating heart. It had been years, outside of dreams and memories.

"Why are you doing this, Simone?" I asked quietly. I knew she'd hear me, even with the sound of the surf behind us. "What did I do to you that made me deserve this? What did Madison do? Or any of those innocent others? When did you become a monster?"

"Always straight to the point as well," she murmured, rolling her eyes. "You did plenty, Sadie. The fact that you don't see it just makes it worse."

I was still walking nearer, but I stopped when she lifted Madison's 'leash' with a warning gaze. I hissed through my extending fangs, but I held my hands up to show that I wasn't going to try anything.

"Maybe you should explain it to me," I growled. "I guess I've been a little *stressed* lately since you've been trying to get me sent up the river for murder and all."

"I knew you'd put that together eventually," she said, waving her free hand.

"But *why*?" I repeated, a little more urgently, emotionally.

Simone shook her head and took a deep breath so she could let out a disappointed sigh. "So smart and yet so stupid."

I bristled but didn't say anything.

"Did you learn anything in all those years we were

together? We helped people, but we stayed to the shadows. How often did I teach you that? How often did I impress upon you the *necessity* of it?"

"We had a different opinion on that," I said, still not seeing the connection. "We always did, I know that and so do you."

"Why didn't you listen to me back then?!" she snapped, her body jerking with her words. I heard a whimper from Madison and started to lunge for her, unable to help myself, but Simone caught back up to herself, and I stopped again.

I kept my arms up, held to my sides, but my hands curled into fists and I felt my nails piercing my skin.

"I always listened," I said, "but that didn't mean I always agreed or went along with what you said. You should remember that too. I'm not one who follows blindly. I was hardly a child when you turned me, and I have always been able to make up my own mind."

She scoffed. Actually scoffed. It wasn't something I saw often and had to note it even now. "I didn't think it would have been following blindly. I thought what happened in Somerset would have been enough to burn it into your mind."

I had to think about that one. Oh, right. We fled a city because we thought our cover had been blown and didn't feel like having our heads chopped off.

"Can we just get to the point? What do I have to do to get my friend back safely?" I was running very low on patience, considering I didn't have much to begin with. It was just one frayed nerve after the other into a cataclysmic failure that was Sadie Stanton.

"Legality," Simone hissed. "You and this bitch's—" She jerked Madison's leash, and my friend cried out. "—brother took away the best protection we all had! Now we are exposed and in the open, and it will take a miracle to make sure that we are all safe again! You have damned us all! How could I not be angry!"

I just stared at her with my mouth open like a fool. My dream came back to me and seemed bizarrely significant. Maybe some part of me knew? I couldn't imagine how I could, but I didn't want to believe it was a coincidence when nothing else was.

The harsh squawk of a seagull overhead snapped me out of my stupor.

"That's what this is all about?" I finally managed to ask.

"Of course!" The way she said it made it seem like I was, in fact, truly stupid for not putting that part together. "Your ideas, your *selfish fantasies*, have put us all at risk forever now."

I blinked and gaped. "Why don't you just stay in the shadows then and leave those of us who want this alone?" I shouted at a decibel level that made Madison and Warren flinch. If it had been any other moment, I would have felt bad.

"Because what would it matter anymore? Once others, like you, are running around talking your heads off, the house of cards falls apart," she spat. She turned her head to stare out over the dark water with an expression of dry sorrow. "All our secrets depend on the secrets of others. We all depend on each other, and you've ruined that for everyone."

"Let Madison go," I said quietly. "If you're mad at me, then be mad at me. I'm here. Let her go. Please."

Simone turned her head back to me with such venom in her gaze that I almost took a step back. Never once in all our years together had she ever looked at me like that. Even those rare times when she got angry, she didn't look like that. She was my sire. She had turned me, brought me into the world of the vampires. A parent, of sorts. How could she look at me with such...hate?

That was the moment I knew I wouldn't talk her out of this. I didn't understand it all, and I realized that I probably couldn't. At this realization, I was filled with such aching sadness.

What had happened to her? What made her this way?

"I guess it's easy to hide behind a hostage," I said, my own fury rising. Rationality wasn't going to work, so I could let myself off my own leash a little. "The Simone I knew would never hide behind someone else like that. You have a fight with me, so come at *me*."

"I'm not the Simone you knew," she hissed. "Just like you aren't the Sadie I knew. You've become weak and ridiculous. Giving in to fantastical notions and trying to force your will on everyone else."

"Oh, my God, would you just shut up? Let it go!"

Words weren't going to work.

I launched across the space between us as quickly as I could, which as a vampire was pretty damn fast. Simone was also a vampire and older than I was, so she was just as quick, but I wasn't going for her...*yet*. Instead, I jumped on the chain. My clothing mostly protected me from the silver as I sent it to the ground. Madison screamed as it dug into her neck, but it was simultaneously ripped out of Simone's grip.

Madison saw this too and bolted just as I picked myself up off the leash, giving her the chance to escape but pausing long enough for Simone to land on my back and send me flat to the rocky sand again. My face stung.

On the upside, I had no wind to be knocked out of me. On the downside, it still hurt like hell as her knees drove down into the small of my back. I shouted in anger and pain, trying to roll her off me but was stopped by her conscious effort. No fledgling is ever stronger than their sire. My only hope was to be smarter.

That was a thought that, honestly, did not fill me with confidence.

A new pain lanced through me as she dug her fingers

into my hair in a classic vampire move and yanked my head to the side. I felt the skin tear off my scalp. When vampires fought, they usually went for the neck—not to feed but to tear apart. I knew her teeth would be coming for me at any moment.

I felt her body weight shifting and knew she was lowering her head. I waited for just a moment and then threw my elbow back as hard as I could. The angle was as uncomfortable as hell, but I gave it all I got. Even vampires don't do well when the hard edge of that joint slams into them.

Her shriek and the sudden lessening of the weight atop me said I'd scored.

It was just enough of a shift for me to push myself up and throw her off. When I looked back, she was holding her eye and spitting a stream of curses likely to light the beach on fire at any moment.

Despite an urge to sit back and be impressed by the breadth of her vocabulary, I chose to capitalize on her distraction instead—smarter, right? I jumped with a tackle that would make any football player proud, driving my shoulder right into her midsection and sending us both tumbling against the boardwalk.

Had she been a human, she'd have been done. She was not, however. Instead of falling in an inglorious pile of limbs, she hit the ground but grabbed my shirt. Somehow using her legs in a way I didn't think should be possible by the laws of science or magic, she actually *threw* me up and over her head. I landed face-first against the edge of the wood and felt my nose break.

All the sensation of tears welled up in me, and I shouted some incomprehensible curse.

I knew I had no time to wallow in the pain, however. I spun around as fast as I could, yet everything felt like it was in slow motion, too. I could actually see thick drops of my blood spray outward in a semi-circle of motion, which—given the lack of a beating heart to move blood through and out of the body—was impressive.

I was right to move fast because I saw her coming for me again. She lunged with her hands out, going for my throat.

Throwing my hands up, I managed to grab one of her wrists. The other got around my neck and squeezed. I felt the sharp points of her nails digging into my skin, so I squeezed the wrist in my hand. I tightened my grip as much as I could and then some. Just shy of her digging her hand too deep into my throat—undoubtedly with a mind to rip my jugular free—I broke the bones of her wrist.

She shrieked at a volume that hurt even my ears and flung herself away from me, cradling her hand to her chest. I could already see the limb at an unnatural angle. She was staggering back, but I didn't intend to let her have any ground. I threw myself to my feet and then straight at her. I pressed my forearm against her neck as I drove her back against the large rock she'd been sitting on, her back bending at a ninety-degree angle. It made a sound that was painful to hear, but I didn't stop.

Her unbroken hand raked at my face and neck, but I held firm. I didn't really have a plan for what to do next, but I knew I had to stop her.

A moment after that, I was nearly blinded by red and blue lights just before strong hands grabbed Simone's flailing arm and held her still.

I looked up to see Dakota holding the vampire while Vance ran down the boardwalk toward us.

CHAPTER TWENTY-FIVE

I stood a little away from the scene of the mayhem with a blanket around my shoulders that I assured them I didn't need. Vampires don't go into physical shock the way humans do, but I suppose I didn't mind it either.

At least my nose had already healed. Being a vampire had its benefits.

There was an ambulance parked up on the road, and I hovered near the door as they loaded Madison into it. *She* looked like she might go into shock, and I was worried about just how much silver exposure she'd received. Immediately after they pulled me and Simone apart, I had seen she'd gotten the silver off from around her neck, but it had burned her neck, hands, and small parts of her face along the way. I just had to hope it was shallow enough and they'd gotten to her soon enough to not leave any lasting effects.

"Can I ride with her?" I asked from the door as they worked on her inside the vehicle.

"You'll have to follow us to the hospital, ma'am," one of the paramedics said apologetically as he shut the door and the ambulance drove off.

"I'll give you a ride," someone said from behind me, and I turned to see Dakota.

I stared at her for a moment. "How'd you know where to find me?"

She smirked and arched a brow. "I was looking for

Warren."

"Right," I said, even though I didn't really feel like that had answered the question, but I didn't have the strength to argue. I looked back and saw the cops standing around the small human scientist asking questions. "What will happen to him?"

"How should I know?" she returned with a shrug. "You'll just have to ask your boyfriend about that."

"He's not—"

"You know I really don't care, right?" She eyed me.

I eyed her back.

She led me to her car, although it was a bit of a walk from where we had been.

"From what I did hear," she finally went on, "the vampire promised to turn him. As it happens, he's not anti-vamp. He's fascinated. Kinda borderline obsessed. He got used."

I didn't have much to say about that except a weary sigh as I got into the passenger's seat of her SUV, and we started off to the hospital. I leaned my head against the window and closed my eyes, letting my thoughts wander for a few moments. I dragged myself back out once I realized my thoughts only wanted to wander into shadow.

"What would you think of working out of my office?" I asked rather abruptly. To be honest, the return of this thought had been equally abrupt, but hey, it was a distraction.

"What?" she asked, clearly as surprised by the timing of my question as I was.

"Like I said, I've been looking to contract a hunter. Maybe we could figure out an arrangement."

She was quiet for a few moments before saying, "I'll think about it."

☾O☽

Madison was still being treated when we arrived, so I found a place in the waiting room. I just hoped they would be done so I could see her before dawn came. Maybe they'd let me sleep in a linen closet or something.

Dakota left to go do...something, and I had some time to sit alone before Vance came walking in. He looked around and then spotted me, coming over to take a seat. "Any word?" he asked.

"Not yet," I said with a sigh.

"I thought you might want to know that Simone had basically confessed to everything before we even got to the car," he went on. "I called the D.A. and they said they'll drop the charges against you, given everything we're getting from her and from Warren. She pretty much held him hostage to make the virus. She hired the Whites and the people who attacked you. Everything. Pretty extensive."

"It's basically like having your mother try to kill you," I said heavily.

He didn't reply right away. I mean, I couldn't blame him. What precisely did you reply to that? I felt his big hand rest on my shoulder.

I should have felt relieved, I knew. The mystery had been solved, and I was off the hook. I wasn't going to prison, and Simone wouldn't be killing anyone else. We knew what had driven the other vampires crazy and how to help if there were any others. I was sure that Madison would be okay because she was getting cared for now.

But I just couldn't feel the relief. Sorrow weighed on me too heavily. I couldn't help but remember all the *good* things Simone and I had done together. I couldn't reconcile the image of her like that versus what I had just faced on the beach.

"Miss Stanton?"

My head snapped up to see a woman in scrubs come through the door looking for me. I jumped to my feet. "Yes?"

The woman smiled kindly. "Miss St John is resting in a room. You can come see her now."

Now, I felt the relief. The sorrow was still there, but all that mattered now was that Madison was going to be okay. I hurried to join the nurse but then paused and looked back at Vance.

"Thank you," I said sincerely.

"Of course," he said, getting to his feet and putting his hands in his pockets. "Are *you* going to be okay?"

"I will be now," I said with a nod and small smile. "I'm going to be fine."

And I knew I would be. It had been a long road so far, but I wouldn't let all of this dissuade me. Ghosts of vampires-past weren't going to set me aside from what I knew to be right. Everything Simone had done and said hurt me deeply, and I knew getting over that wound would take a while, but she hadn't achieved her goal. She could not convince me Cameron's Law and the path of legality was wrong.

I was a vampire, and I was going to live my life in the light now.

Well, in the moonlight, at least.

AUTHOR'S NOTE

I originally published this story, at least conceptually, as *This Shade of Night* by K. Parlin back in...2003. It was part of the Preternatural, Unlimited Series back then, and I was around nineteen. I published it through iUniverse. Anyone remember them? I had to pay to have it done. I didn't sell much, but I got a decent review in a publisher trade journal. I went running and screaming around the house.

That seems like so long ago now.

It quietly went away, but I kept writing. I had my son in 2010, and after I recovered from that, I decided that I wanted to live my best life to give my son his best life and show him to live your dreams. That's when I really got serious about being an author. I released a heavily revised/totally rewritten version of this as *Cameron's Law* in 2011 by Mia Darien, the first book in the Adelheid Series.

Life moved and changed. I moved and changed. I started freelancing in addition to writing and publishing, but somewhere along the way, it all got muddy for me. I'm still trying to figure out what happened, but while it was happening, the self-publishing world changed on me. And my freelancing overlapped too much with my author stuff.

It was time for a change. I had to reinvent myself as well as this, my 'flagship' series. The one I've loved the most and for the longest. I had to separate Author Me from Freelancing Me and try to keep up with the publishing world as it is now.

That's what brings us here.

Why Blood Rights? As you've read in this book, the whole series deals with civil rights for preternatural beings. Vampires like blood. The blood of a supernatural is different. A twist on the phrase *blood rites*... And there you are. Previously, you couldn't really tell from title or cover that these were urban fantasy. I've been fixing that. I revised this book a lot from its last version to be better and respond to critiques in previous reviews, so the story stands by itself better as well as becomes a gateway to the rest of the series.

So... Welcome to Adelheid, and the reinvention of an author. I hope you enjoy your time in my city as much as I do. Sadie and Dakota especially have been part of my head and life for nearly twenty years. I hope you enjoy their snark!

If you want to know more about the town of Adelheid, the people who live in it, and the lore I chose to use when writing these preternatural species, you can check out my series wiki at wiki.authorkbthorne.com.

Sincerely,

K. B. Thorne, July 2020

ABOUT THE AUTHOR

Born a Connecticut Yankee in nobody's court, K. B. Thorne grew up to brave snow and talk fast.

She started reading when she was three and never looked back, soon frequently falling asleep with a book under her cheek. At eleven, she discovered *Night Mare* by Piers Anthony and entered the world of grown-up fantasy fiction. As you can guess, it was all over from there. She started writing at fourteen, then met vampires as a teenager and the concept for what would become Adelheid (now the Blood Rights Series) was soon born. Mia Darien followed a few years later, and the books were released.

However, K. B. is also a third-generation Trekkie. Somewhere in a vault at Paramount is a very angry letter written by her grandmother when *Star Trek: The Original Series* was cancelled, so sci-fi is in the blood too. Alongside a love of love and an adoration for her first love of epic fantasy.

K. B. Thorne is the evolution of Mia Darien after years of learning and living. She has taken both of those things to become a smarter, better writer with a fresh new face and take on the literary world. Thorne writes the urban fantasy, fantasy and sci-fi, while Sadie Johnston writes the romance.

These days, when she's not desperately trying to find time to write, she works as a freelance editor/cover artist/formatter and happily lives her unconventional life alongside her very own Named Man of the North and their mini-tank. (Who is, you know, their son.)

You can find K. B. at authorkbthorne.com!

OTHER BOOKS
BY K. B. THORNE

Writing as K. B. Thorne
Blood Rights Series

Bad Blood
Blood and Thunder
Blood Moon
Written in Blood
Bloodshot
First Blood
Out for Blood
New Blood
Flesh and Blood

Out for Blood Series
Bones & Blood

Bellator (Anthology)
Good Things (Anthology)
Ashes to Sunrise (Anthology)
The Shape of Tomorrow (Anthology)
Born of Defiance (Anthology)

Writing as Sadie Johnston (Romance)
Beauty
Help Wanted (with Viola Dawn)
Threnody (with Alastair Malone)
Here, Kitty Kitty (Anthology)
Amor Vincit Omnia (Anthology)
Second Chances (Anthology)